Business Is Business

A NOVEL

SILK WHITE

Good 2 Go Publishing

Books by This Author

Business Is Business

Married To Da Streets

Never Be The Same

Stranded

Tears of a Hustler

Tears of a Hustler 2

Tears of a Hustler 3

Tears of a Hustler 4

Tears of a Hustler 5

Tears of a Hustler 6

Teflon Queen

Teflon Queen 2

Teflon Queen 3

Teflon Queen 4

Time Is Money (An Anthony Stone Novel)

48 Hours to Die (An Anthony Stone Novel)

Copyright © 2015 by Good2Go Publishing

ISBN: 978-0-9908694-7-4

Published 2015 by Good2Go Publishing
7311 W. Glass Lane, Laveen, AZ 85339
www.good2gopublishing.com
Twitter @good2gobooks
G2G@good2gopublishing.com
Facebook.com/good2gopublishing
ThirdLane Marketing: Brian James
Brian@good2gopublishing.com

Cover Design: Davida Baldwin
Editor: Kesha Buckhana

Printed in the United States of America

AUG - - 2015

Acknowledgments

To all of you who are reading this, thank you for stepping inside the bookstore, stopping by the library, or downloading a copy of Business is Business. I hope you have enjoyed this read from top to bottom. My goal is to get better and better with each story. I want to thank everyone for all their love and support. It is definitely appreciated! Now without further ado Ladies and Gentleman, I give you *Business Is Business.*

BUSINESS IS BUSINESS

JIMMY

1

Jimmy Mason stood in his hotel suite staring out the window at the beautiful night view that New York City had to offer. He was dressed in a navy blue tailored Armani suit. In one hand was a glass of Cîroc and in the other was a 9mm. Gathered in the room along with Jimmy was his driver-slash-bodyguard, Big Foot. He got the name Big Foot because he was a huge man with a quick temper and a bad attitude. If you were a friend or family of Big Foot, he was one of the nicest people that one would ever meet. But if you were an enemy of the big man, he would become your worst nightmare.

Jimmy downed his drink and quickly poured himself another shot when he heard a loud knock at the door. He looked over at Big Foot and nodded letting him know it was okay for him to answer the door. Big Foot opened the door and stepped to the side as two rough looking men entered the room.

"Hey Jimmy what's with the surprise meeting?" The shorter one out of the two whose name was Malcolm asked.

The taller one whose name was Marcus followed up, "I thought we weren't supposed to meet again until next week?"

"Gentlemen have a seat," Jimmy said in a calm tone. He then nodded at Big Foot signaling for him to remove their weapons. Once that was done, Jimmy began. "I've been hearing some interesting things out on these streets," he said letting his gun rest freely at his side. He then looked directly at Malcolm. "Word on the streets is that you've been real friendly with the cops lately, something you want to tell me?"

Malcolm had a nervous I'm busted look on his face. "Jimmy who told you that?"

"Fuck who told me, is it true?" Jimmy barked aiming his 9mm at, Malcolm's head.

"The Mason family has been nothing but good to me I would never do something like that," Malcolm said with a frightened look on his face. He had been getting supplied by the Mason family for years and knew exactly how they dealt with a problem. "Your father, Derrick Mason was the one who gave me my start out here in these streets."

Jimmy held his 9mm aimed at, Malcolm's head when he heard another knock at the door. He gave Big Foot a nod and watched as he answered the door. When the handsome light skin man walked in the hotel room, Malcolm looked like he had just seen a ghost. "I would like for you to meet my adopted brother Detective Mike Brown," Jimmy said with a smile on his face. Jimmy's father Derrick Mason adopted Mike when he was a kid and treated him like his own, but instead of letting him join the family business he forced him into the police academy, now years later. Mike was one of the best and most respected detective's in the city and since his last name wasn't Mason, it made it easier for him to play both sides of the coin without anyone finding out.

"Nice to see you again," Mike smiled while looking at, Malcolm. "Malcolm here has been cooperating with police for the last three weeks trying to bring down the Mason family, isn't that right, Malcolm?"

"Listen, Jimmy I can explain," Malcolm said in a fast pitch tone as his head forcefully snapped to the left from a powerful punch from, Big Foot.

"What about him?" Jimmy turned his gun on, Marcus. "Is he snitching too?"

"Nah Marcus is a standup guy unlike his brother here," Mike said with a disgusted look on his face.

"Come here!" Jimmy said looking at, Marcus. "You want to keep your life?"

"Yes, Jimmy," Marcus said with fear in his eyes. He knew that, Jimmy was the enforcer in the Mason family and loved to inflict pain on people. When people spoke about Jimmy they always attached his violent reputation to whatever story was being told at the time.

Jimmy grabbed a gun from off the table and handed it to Marcus. "Kill, Malcolm if you want to keep your life."

"But, Malcolm is my brother," Marcus said looking up at Jimmy.

Jimmy took a few steps closer invading, Marcus's personal space. "You consigning for this snitch?"

Marcus looked into Jimmy's eyes and shook his head as he slowly took the pistol from Jimmy's hand and aimed it at his brother Malcolm's head.

"Marcus don't do this," Malcolm pleaded as tears ran down his face. "I made an honest mistake please don't do this," he begged. "You do this and mommy will never forgive you, we're brothers."

Marcus held the pistol aimed at his brother's head as warm tears slowly slid down his face.

"Marcus please don't do this I thought you were your brother's keeper?" Malcolm pleaded.

"I am," Marcus whispered as he pulled the trigger and watched his brother's brains pop out the back of his skull. He then fired two more shots into his brother's already dead body. "If it's one thing I can't stand is a snitch."

"You did good," Big Foot said as he slowly removed the gun from, Marcus's hand.

Marcus took a deep breath. "I love my brother to death but I wasn't raised to snitch on no..."

"Boom!

Marcus's body crumbled down to the floor face first as Jimmy stood behind him holding a smoking gun.

"Damn it!" Mike spat. "That was totally unnecessary!"

"I did us a favor," Jimmy said holstering his weapon. "What you think he was just going to let us slide for making him murder his own brother?"

"Marcus was a stand up dude you didn't have to do that!" Mike spat getting up in Jimmy's face. He hated Jimmy's hot temper and his shoot first and ask questions later mentality.

"How can you trust a man that just killed his own brother?" Jimmy asked with his face crumbled up. "If he killed his own brother what the fuck you think he would have done to one of us given the chance?"

Mike thought about it for a second and left it alone. "I'm not cleaning this up," he said as he exited the hotel room leaving Jimmy and Big Foot alone in their own thoughts.

DERRICK

2

Derrick Mason sat in the entertainment area of his mansion watching several football games that all played at the same time. He was the leader and head of the Mason Family as well as the brains behind their successful operation. Derrick looked through the surveillance camera and saw Mike entering his home through the back door. Even though Mike was adopted, Derrick treated him no different from his two other sons, Jimmy and Eric. Derrick looked up and saw Mike enter the entertainment area with his face crumbled up.

"Pop we need to talk," Mike said as he grabbed the bottle of tequila and poured himself a shot. "It's, Jimmy, he's out of control."

"I heard about what happened," Derrick said pouring himself a drink. "But you do have to remember that Jimmy is the enforcer in the family."

"Pop he's going to get us all put in jail if he continues with the unnecessary killings," Mike pointed out. "And on top of that he did it inside one of the rooms at your hotel bringing heat toward one of our biggest assets."

"I'll have a talk with him," Derrick downed his drink in one gulp. "We all play a big part in this family business. Jimmy's job is to enforce, your job is to make sure that you give me the heads up if any heat ever starts to come down on us or let us know if any rivals crew ever have any big deals going down. Eric's job is to keep his nose clean and keep acquiring us more and more assets so we can hide more and more money and my job is to keep the money rolling in, oversee everything, and keep everyone out of jail we have a good system going here."

"I understand pop but can you just please have a talk with him, maybe tell him to calm down just a little because that would definitely make my job a lot easier."

Derrick looked up and saw Eric and his wife Kelly making their way towards the entertainment area. "I'll talk to him," he extended his hand.

Mike looked at Derrick's hand for a long second before he finally shook it. "Thank you I better get going," he said as he headed for the back exit. He had to keep a low profile and not risk someone being able to identify or affiliate him with the Mason Family.

"Hey pop," Eric gave his father a hug.

"Hey son how are you?" Derrick smiled then turned his attention to, Kelly. "Hey, Kelly," he placed a kiss on her cheek.

"Hey, Derrick," Kelly said with a smile as her and Eric helped themselves to a seat. Kelly was a beautiful white woman with a nice body and long blonde hair that stopped at the middle of her back. She and Eric had been married for four years now, but during the years, the two definitely had their ups and downs.

"Got a few things I need to talk to you about pop," Eric began. "I found two apartment buildings

I had my eye on I think they can bring in some real money."

"I'm glad you said that son I've been thinking," Derrick paused and glanced at Kélly.

"I'm going to go make me something to eat," Kelly got up quickly dismissing herself so the two men could talk privately.

"I want you to purchase those two apartment buildings," Derrick said with a grin.

"Great because with both of those buildings we should be able to bring in at least two to three million a year, so I was thinking..."

"We'll let tenants rent out all the apartments in one building and we'll turn the other building into a trap house," Derrick cut him off. "We can use that entire building as a stash house for all of our product."

"Pop I thought you wanted me to find great investments for us so soon we could get out of the drug business and go legit?" Eric said not understanding. "I thought that was the whole purpose of me going to college all those years and you keeping me away from the drugs?" Eric didn't understand his father, they had way more than enough money to never sell another drug again but yet and still here he was risking his and the entire family's freedom to continue to feed the streets with drugs.

"Son, it's my job to run this family and that's what I'm doing," Derrick said pouring himself another drink. "You can never have enough money son. Never."

"Money's not everything pop."

"How dare you say something foolish like that?" Derrick spat. "It was drug money that paid for you to go to college, it was also drug money that paid for that huge house you live in, not to mention the BMW and Range Rover that you and your wife drive."

Eric looked at his father with a disgusted look on his face. "I don't care about material things they come and go but what about the things that money can't buy?"

"With enough money one can buy, pay for, or name a price for just about anything," Derrick smiled.

"Well then why is mom still in jail since money can buy anything, why haven't you brought her freedom yet?" Eric challenged. For the past seven years, his mother had been incarcerated for some serious drug charges. But instead of ratting on the family for a shorter sentence, Mildred Mason took her time like a soldier.

Derrick downed his drink. "Millie was a good woman and a great mother, but she knew the risk just like the rest of us."

"She's got caught with your drugs and she's in jail because she didn't snitch on you and how do you repay her by sleeping with different women every night, when's the last time you even went to see her?" Eric asked.

"I make sure that Millie has everything that she needs and you know it," Derrick countered. "Me going to see her won't help her out with her early release, if everything goes according to plan with good behavior she'll be out in two years," Derrick poured two drinks and handed one to Eric, but he quickly refused because he didn't drink, smoke, or put anything in his system that wasn't healthy. "Don't worry about your mother she'll be well taken care of for the rest of her life and she knows that. Millie is a soldier there's not even a lot of men that's built like her."

"All I'm saying is when is enough going to be enough, how many more millions do we need?" Eric asked. "We make millions every year just from all the assets we've accumulated sometimes it's best to get out the game on your own instead of being forced out the game."

Derrick sipped his drink and shook his head. Ever since Eric was a kid, he'd always been soft. While other kids were playing football, he was in the house reading a book, when other kids his age got into girls he was into learning how the stock market worked and operated. Ever since he was a kid, he had been different. "All I need is a little more time and we will go a hundred percent legit I promise."

"I just don't want all of us to wind up in a jail cell when this is all said and done."

Derrick nodded. "All I need is a little bit more time," he extended his hand. "You trust me?"

Eric shook his father's hand. "Of course I do."

JIMMY

3

"Pull over right here, I think this the restaurant right here," Jimmy said from the back seat. He had been running around all day and every time he got ready to unwind, it seemed like the family business kept calling which wasn't unusual. Big Foot parked in front of the five-star restaurant, stepped out the driver seat, and opened the back door for Jimmy.

Jimmy stepped out the back of the Range Rover dressed in an expensive burgundy tailored suit. His swagger was on another level as he walked in the restaurant like he own the place because his father really did own the place. Women were known to say that him and the rapper Nas could have been twins the only difference between the two men were that Jimmy had a little bit more bulk to his already muscular frame.

Jimmy and Big Foot entered the restaurant and they were immediately met by the manager.

"Sorry to have to call you on such short noticed but I didn't know who else to call," the manager said with a scared look on her face. She was a blonde woman who looked to be in her early forties with pearly white teeth.

"What seems to be the problem?" Jimmy asked already in a bad mood.

"Well it's this guy, him and his partner come in here almost every other day," the manager began. "But when it's time to pay the tab there's always a problem and it never gets paid."

"How much does he owe?"

"Seven thousand dollars."

"Seven thousand dollars?" Jimmy echoed with a raised brow. "Why haven't you called me?"

"I didn't want any trouble," the manager said honestly. "These guys definitely strike me as the trouble-making type."

"Okay so where are these guys now?"

"All the way in the back last booth on the left," the manager said with a scared look on her face as she watched Jimmy and Big Foot head towards the back of the restaurant.

Jimmy walked up to the last booth on the left and spotted two Mexican looking men sitting in a booth across from two white chicks who's breast looked to be the size of balloons. "Good evening gentlemen," Jimmy said politely. "I was told by the manager that you guys had a problem with the bill?"

The two Mexican men continued on with their conversation with the two white chicks like the men standing in front of their table was invisible.

Without warning, Jimmy snatched the two white girls out of the booth by their hair and violently tossed them down to the floor. The two Mexican men went to get up but stopped when they saw the big cannon that Big Foot had aimed at them.

"Your tab is seven thousand!" Jimmy spat. "Pay it then get the fuck out!"

The Mexican men looked unfazed as they looked at Jimmy as if he was retarded. "You must not know who we are. We are the Ricardo brothers," the oldest one said like that was supposed to mean something.

"I don't give a fuck all I care about is you paying your tab," Jimmy said, he was two seconds away from losing his cool.

The two Mexican men didn't budge. Jimmy sighed loudly as he spun on his heels. "Excuse me can I get everyone's attention I'm going to need everyone to head towards the exit!" He announced. It took about seven minutes until the restaurant was finally empty. Jimmy then walked to the back kitchen then returned carrying a wooden baseball bat in his hand. He stared at the oldest for a second then swung the baseball bat with all his might until it connected with the Mexican man's head making a loud cracking sound as blood splattered all over the wall and windows. Jimmy swung the bat repeatedly beating the Mexican man as if he was a Piñata. Jimmy then turned his focus on the next brother.

"No please I'll pay," he said with his hands raised in an *I surrender* gesture.

"Oooooh," Jimmy laughed as he faced Big Time. "Now this motherfucker can speak English," without warning, Jimmy turned and hit a home run with the Mexican's head. Big Foot laughed as he watched, Jimmy beat the Mexican man to a bloody pulp.

Jimmy's chest rose up and down as he breathed heavily while resting his arms for a second. "I see you ain't talking shit now," he tossed the baseball bat down to the floor. "Call up the cleaning people and have them clean this mess up," Jimmy said then exited the restaurant. Outside he pulled out his cell phone and dialed a number the phone rung four times before someone finally answered it. "What's good? Can you get out tonight? A'ight cool meet me at my crib in an hour, a'ight one."

Big Foot pulled up in front of Jimmy's huge estate and placed the gear in park. "You gon be alright for the night?"

"Yeah I'm calling it a night," Jimmy leaned over and bumped fist with Big Foot. "I'll holla at you in the A.M."

"But if you need me I'm just one call away," Big Foot made sure that Jimmy made it inside safe before he pulled off.

Jimmy removed his suit jacket and noticed it had bloodstains on it. "Damn I should go back and kill those clowns again for messing up my suit." He walked over to the kitchen and poured himself a strong drink as he heard someone ringing his doorbell. "Who is it?" Jimmy yelled when he got close to the door.

"It's me," the voice on the other end of the door yelled out.

Jimmy opened the door and looked his guest up and down. "Took you long enough."

Kelly stepped inside Jimmy's house and wrapped her arms around his neck. "Sorry baby but I had a hard time getting out of the house tonight. Your brother was on my back like a cheap suit."

"I don't know what you doing with a square like that anyway," Jimmy hated. "When you going to tell him about us?"

"In due time baby," Kelly said as her and Jimmy shared a long sloppy kiss. Jimmy reached down and felt that Kelly didn't have on any draws.

"Just how I like it," Jimmy smiled devilishly as he scooped, Kelly up in his arms and carried her over to the counter where he spread her legs apart and began to slowly kiss on her inner thighs until he made his way up to her clit.

Kelly threw her head back and let out a loud moan as she grabbed the back of Jimmy's head forcing his face even further into her wetness. The one thing she loved about Jimmy was how aggressive he was, and she loved a man that knew how to take control. When dealing with Eric, she always had to be the one in control and that was a super turn off in her book.

Once Jimmy was done orally pleasing Kelly, he roughly snatched her off the counter and bent her over. "Grab your ankles," he growled slapping her ass so hard that it left a handprint. "I said grab your ankles now!"

"Yes daddy," Kelly bit down on her bottom lip as she spread her legs and seductively bent down and grabbed her ankles. She moaned loudly as she felt Jimmy forcefully enter her from behind.

Jimmy plunged in and out of Kelly at a quick and fast pace. He fucked her as if he was trying to punish her instead of please her, he fucked her like the world was coming to an end and this would be his last chance to ever be with a woman again. He grabbed a hand full of, Kelly's hair and forcefully jerked her head back. "Who pussy is this?"

"It's yours," she moaned.

"I can't hear you!" He slacked her ass.

"It's yours!"

"I can't hear you!" Jimmy slapped her ass again but this time even harder.

"It's yours daddy! Oh daddy it's all yours!" Kelly yelled.

Jimmy delivered four more strokes, and then quickly pulled out, and spun Kelly around forcing her down to her knees then painted her face with his fluids. "Argh yeah baby you like that don't you?"

Kelly nodded her head. "Yes daddy."

KELLY

4

Kelly pulled into her drive way and killed the engine; she glanced down at her watch and saw that it was 3:15 am. "Shit!" She cursed loudly mad that she let to the time slip away from her like that. She knew sleeping with two bothers was wrong, but it felt so good. Kelly looked down at her phone and noticed she had four missed calls from Eric. She stepped foot inside her home and noticed that it was quiet hopefully that meant, Eric was sleep and she wouldn't have to hear his mouth until the morning. Kelly entered her bedroom and found Eric sitting up in the bed wide-awake.

"Where have you been?" Eric asked not even bothering to look at Kelly.

"Oh hey baby," Kelly, said fumbling over her words. "What are you doing up?"

"Where were you?" Eric repeated, but this time in a deadly tone.

"Baby I was at my mother's house," Kelly said, spitting out the first thing that came to her mind. "She wasn't feeling too good so I went over there to make sure she was alright."

"So you couldn't pick up your phone and tell me that?" Eric's asked with a raised brow. "I hop in the shower and when I got out you were gone, then I call you several times, and you don't answer."

"Sorry baby my phone was on vibrate and I didn't hear it," Kelly lied. "Come here baby," she grabbed Eric and placed his head on her breast as she hugged him. "I'm sorry baby but when I got the call from my mother I got worried and ran straight over there I promise it will never happen again."

Eric looked Kelly in the eyes and gave her a long wet kiss. "What's this?"

"What?"

"You have some white stuff next to your mouth," he said scratching the crust from off the side of Kelly's mouth with his fingernail.

"Oh, I ate a glazed donut while I was at my mother's house I must have got some of the frosting on my mouth," she giggled then headed to the bathroom. Inside the bathroom, Kelly grabbed a washcloth and scrubbed her face making sure none of Jimmy's left overs were on her face. "That was a close one," she looked up at her reflection in the mirror and smirked.

DERRICK

5

"Sure Mr. Alvarez. I apologize, I'll be over to see you tonight so we can fix this situation," Derrick said. "And again, Mr. Alvarez I apologize," he said then hung up the phone. Derrick looked up from his office chair at, Jimmy who on the opposite side of his desk. "What the hell is wrong with you? Do you have any idea what you've done?"

"Pop it wasn't my fault all I was trying to do was..."

"Shut your mouth!" Derrick shot to his feet. "You and your hot headed ways are going to bring this family down!"

"Pop I was only doing my job," Jimmy tried to explain.

"You killed two men over six thousand dollars," Derrick growled.

"It was seven thousand," Jimmy corrected him and was rewards with a strong slap to his face.

"You acting like a stupid hot headed nigga!" Derrick spat. "You know the difference between being a nigga and being a Mason?" He continued not giving his son a chance to answer. "A nigga is a person that will shoot somebody for stepping on their shoe, or kill a person over something petty over, something that could of been talked out," he paused. "And a Mason is a business man, a man with integrity, a man that runs multimillion dollar companies. Son you are a million dollar man and yet you out here killing people over seven thousand dollars; what sense does that make? You have to be smarter than that."

"I fucked up," Jimmy said with his head hung low. He was known for taking things to the extreme but even he had to admit that his father was right.

"Those two men that you killed were the Ricardo brothers. Do you even know who they are?" Derrick asked sitting on the edge of his desk.

"No," Jimmy answered with a dumb look on his face. Truth be told he really didn't care who the two Mexican men were they violated and got dealt with end of the story.

"The Ricardo brothers were made men," Derrick explained. "They worked as enforcers for the Alvarez family."

"Shit!" Jimmy cursed. He knew all about the Alvarez family. They controlled the drug trade in Brooklyn, Queens, and Staten Island. While the Mason family controlled the drug trade in Harlem, the Bronx, and Yonkers. "I'm sorry pop I didn't know."

"Start using your head," Derrick jabbed his finger in the center of Jimmy's forehead.

"So what now do we go to war with the Alvarez family?" Jimmy asked.

"I have to meet with Joey Alvarez tonight and see if I can somehow smooth this thing over," Derrick shook his head. He knew something like this wouldn't be able to be resolved easily, the Ricardo brothers were made men, and made men were considered untouchable. Doing harm to a made man was like committing suicide, if one wanted to harm or kill a made man he needed permission to do so. "Please start using your head out here son your actions can hurt this entire family."

"I'm sorry pop."

"Me and your mother worked too hard to get this family where it is today," he paused. "And I'm not going to sit back and let you ruin it," Derrick said in a deadly tone.

"I understand pop I promise you something like this will never happen again."

"Now leave me," Derrick said in a dismissive manner as he went and sat back behind his desk. Derrick had a lot to think about and didn't want to be disturbed.

MIKE

6

Mike sat in the classroom full of detective's and his fellow officers. The captain had called in an emergency meeting. Mike didn't know what was going on, but whatever it was, it had to be big. Minutes later, the captain stepped in the room and all the chatter and laughing ceased.

"Good afternoon gentlemen," The captain began. "I'm not going to keep you all here long so I'm going to get straight to it," he said as he walked over to the wall and hit the lights, another officer then turned on the projector. On the huge projector screen was a photo of Derrick Mason. "This here is Derrick Mason he's in charge and controls the drug trade in Harlem and the Bronx, he and his family are responsible for over one hundred murders in the last three years," the captain paused for a second giving his words a chance to sink in. "As with any monster you hit the head and the body will crumble," he pointed at Derrick Mason's photo. "This here ladies and gentlemen is the head."

"What about the rest of the family?" Mike asked. He wanted to see how much dirt they had on the rest of the family as well.

"Glad you asked," the captain smiled as he removed Derrick's photo and replaced it with Jimmy's photo. "This here ladies and gentlemen is Jimmy Mason the family's enforcer. From what I hear, this guy is supposedly a real gunslinger and action freak. Whenever approaching him please do so with caution because nine times out of time he'll be strapped and ready to bang at a moment's notice," he removed, Jimmy's photo and replaced it with Eric's photo. "This here is Eric Mason he's the brains of the operation and also the money man. He takes all of the Mason's family illegal money and turns it into legal money by buying up any piece of real estate he can get his hands on, he's a very wise man, and good at what he does. Eric has made some wonderful investments for the Mason family over the years, but their run is about to be over real soon because as of today we have the green light to get the Mason family off the streets. Operation shut down is in full affect," the captain smiled. "Let's go find some dirt and evidence on the Mason family and get them off the streets once and for all."

Once the meeting was over, Mike pulled out his cell phone and walked out into the hallway, he slipped a different chip in his phone then sent Derrick a text message that said "666" the code that meant the devil is on the way.

DERRICK

7

Derrick sat in the back of his Maybach with the curtains closed enjoying a stiff drink. In the seat next to him was his personal bodyguard, a big baldhead man that went by the name Tony. Derrick had no clue how this night was going to play out all he could do was hope and pray that Jimmy's actions didn't get a contract put on his head. Derrick sipped his drink when he felt his cell phone vibrating on his hip he looked down at the screen and saw Millie's name flashing across the screen. At the moment, he didn't really feel like talking to her, but for the past two weeks, he had been avoiding her calls. "Hey baby," he answered.

"Hey baby my ass where the fuck you been I know you seen me calling you," Millie snapped.

"Sorry baby it's been crazy out here," Derrick began. "How you been though?"

"I been good, I'm going to need you to send another girl up here with another package. These girls in here been going crazy for this new shit," Millie laughed.

"Damn you finished that package already?" Derrick smiled. The one thing he knew about his wife was that she was a hustler. Once a month, Derrick had a random chick go up to the jail and drop off a package for Millie; he paid several of the correctional officers not to bother Millie and let her do as she pleased. In returned, Millie charged the girl inside triple then sent the money back home. "You don't play no games."

"You know I love money," Millie smiled. "How are the boys?"

"They're good," Derrick sighed. "You know that damn Jimmy is going to give me more gray hairs."

"How's my baby, Eric?" Millie asked. Ever since Eric was a baby that was always her favorite. She vowed that she wouldn't expose him to the family business or any other illegal activities. "You still keeping his hands and record clean?"

"Yes of course you know I would never taint your golden child," Derrick teased. He knew how Millie felt about Eric.

"What have you been up too?"

"Working my ass off."

"You miss me?" Millie sat on her bed, removed her pants and panties.

"Like crazy," Derrick growled as he sipped his drink.

"What about this pussy, do you miss her too?" Millie licked her fingers, spread her legs, and began rubbing pussy lips in a slow circular motion.

"You have no idea."

"Tell me what you going to do to her when "we" get out of here," she said in a deep sexy phone operator type voice.

"First I'm going to talk to her, and then I'm going to kiss her. Then I'm going to tie your hands up so you can't stop me from going crazy on that pussy," Derrick said in a growl. "Then I'm going to lick her nice and slow, then once you get into it I'm going to stop, look at her, spit on her then lick it all up. I'm going to be slurping on that pussy so loud it's going to sound like a kid just finished eating cereal and drinking the milk from bowl."

"Aww, yes eat that pussy daddy," Millie moaned in a light whisper while her fingers moved a hundred miles per second. "I'm cuming daddy, I'm cuming!"

"Mmmm... yes make that pussy cum for daddy," Derrick said making loud slurping noises with his mouth until Millie's orgasm took over. "I love you baby I gotta go dream about me," he blew her a kiss then hung up. Derrick turned and looked at Tony who sat there pretending as if he was looking at something important on his phone. "Sorry about that, had to take care of my wife real quick."

"No problem," Tony said as the Maybach pulled into the Alvarez family estate. The mansion looked like three high schools could fit inside. The driver walked around to the back of the vehicle and held the door open as, Derrick stepped out the back seat in a three thousand dollar suit and a cigar in his mouth. His light skin and smooth baldhead not to mention his million-dollar smile was his best asset. Derrick favored the rap mogul Dame Dash.

"Gentlemen right this way," the doorman said escorting Derrick through the mansion. It seemed as if the three men were walking forever when Derrick spotted four big bodyguards dressed in all black. He and Tony were immediately searched and removed of their weapons.

"Derrick Mason," Joey Alvarez smiled as he stood and shook Derrick's hand. Joey poured two drinks and handed one to Derrick.

"Let me start off by apologizing for my son and his actions," Derrick sipped his drink.

Joey sipped his drink. "Your son didn't know that the Ricardo brothers were made men?" He asked with a raised brow. "I find that hard to believe."

"I apologize for my son and his ignorance," Derrick said again. "It was an honest mistake there has to be a way we can fix this."

"You kill a made man and the consequences are death you know that Derrick," Joey said in a calm tone. "Besides from what I hear your son has been out there bringing a lot of heat down on the entire city with his wild cowboy antics."

"I know, Jimmy has been a handful but I can personally promise you if you give him another chance I'll keep him in check," Derrick pleaded.

"I don't know Derrick, your boy seems to be out of control," Joey sipped his drink. "He may have to be put down."

Derrick sipped his drink then smiled. "Listen Joey, I have a lot of respect for you and your family but Jimmy is my son and I'm not going to just sit back and let you take my boy from me."

"Then the next step is a war," Joey said in his usual calm tone. "This is not up for negotiations your son broke the rules plain and simple and he will be dealt with accordingly."

"Before we declare an all-out war and mess up both of our money I'm asking that you rethink this because this isn't going to end good for either side,"

Derrick stated plainly. "Give my son another chance...please."

"One million dollars and you owe me two favors take it or leave it," Joey sipped his drink. He was going to spare Jimmy's life because he had a lot of respect for Derrick.

"I'll take it," Derrick said quickly.

"Great," Joey smiled. "For the first favor there's this guy out in Florida that snitched on a cousin of mines," he paused to sip his drink again. "I want you to take care of him."

"Done," Derrick stood to his feet and extended his hand. "I'll have the million dollars delivered to you first thing in the morning."

"You're a good man, Derrick," Joey shook his hand. "Keep an eye on that son of yours he's going to have you in a cell if he keeps it up."

"I'll get the money to you first thing in the morning," Derrick turned and made his exit.

Once Derrick and Tony slid in the back of the Maybach, Derrick unleashed a series of curses. "A million fucking dollars can you believe that cock sucker?"

"I'm not trying to tell you what to do, but if you pay Joey he's going to think he owns you," Tony said. "You know how those old mob type guys are."

"Going to war with the Alvarez family and we're sure to lose millions of dollars due to all the heat that's going to come down," Derrick explained. "I'm going to pay him and keep it moving," he fumed. "You get Jimmy on the phone and let him know I need to see him first thing in the morning!"

"You got it boss," Tony said. He didn't like how things were playing out, he saw nothing good coming from paying Joey Alvarez but it wasn't his call to make so he just kept quiet. Tony sat back staring out the window when he noticed the driver make a sudden detour once he saw what street they were headed down he already knew what time it was.

"Third house on the left pull into the drive way," Derrick ordered. The driver pulled into the driveway, stepped out the vehicle, walked around the back, and held the door open for, Derrick.

"I'll holla at you in the morning," Derrick said as he bumped fist with Tony.

"You sure you gon alright for the night?" Tony asked.

"I'm good now go home and get you some rest," Derrick said as he slammed the door shut and watched as the Maybach's tail lights disappeared down the street. He then quickly walked up to the front door and rang the doorbell. Seconds later a sexy light skin woman with blonde hair answered the door wearing nothing but a silk Chinese robe that was left wide open.

"Damn Pearl," Derrick licked his lips. "Hey baby."

"Get in here!" Pearl growled as she reached out and snatched Derrick inside her house. For the past five years, Pearl and Derrick been going strong. What started out as friendly sex turned into a full-blown relationship. Now Pearl was doing everything in her power to try and get Derrick to get a divorce. "It took you long enough to get here," Pearl said. She removed her robe and let it him the floor. "You gon stand there all night or you gon come get This pussy?" Pearl spun and headed towards the bedroom, her bright red pumps stabbed the hard wood floor with each step she took.

Derrick stood with a grin on his face as he watched, Pearl's huge ass jiggle with each step she took. Without thinking twice, Derrick followed Pearl in the bedroom and shut the door behind him.

ERIC

8

Eric sat in the booth at a five-star restaurant with a scowl on his face. Once again, his wife had disappeared, and then showed up hours later trying to down play her disappearance. It was beginning to become a pattern. Eric wanted to give his wife the benefit of the doubt but some things just weren't adding up. He sipped his wine and said, "So you ready to tell me where you've been sneaking off to in the middle of the night?"

Kelly rolled her eyes and let out a loud sigh. "Could you not start tonight please I already have a headache."

"No I'm not going to let it go!" Eric said his voice projecting louder than he had meant for it to.

"Let it go Eric," Kelly said giving him the evil eye. The truth was she didn't know how to tell Eric that she was sleeping with his brother. Kelly found herself falling in love with them both and enjoyed the fact that she could have her cake and eat it too. "You are so jealous for no reason; you're going to have to trust me and learn to respect my privacy."

"I do respect your privacy, but you disappearing for hours is unacceptable!" Eric barked.

"Lower your voice!"

"Where have you been disappearing to?" Eric growled.

"You've had way too much to drink," Kelly said gathering her things. "Come on its time for us to go."

"I'm not going nowhere with you," Eric looked his wife up and down as if she was a piece of trash. "Go crawl back under the rock that you came from," he flicked his wrist in a dismissive manner.

Kelly grabbed her drink off the table and tossed it in Eric's face.

Splash!

"Asshole!" She stood to her feet and stormed out the restaurant leaving Eric sitting there covered in wine. Eric grabbed his handkerchief and cleaned the wine from his face and suit. Immediately he felt horrible for the way he spoke to his wife, he quickly ran outside to try and catch her but when he made it out to the front of the restaurant it was too late. Kelly was already long gone. "Shit!" He cursed. Eric hurried over to his B.M.W. trying to catch his wife before she made it back home. He pulled out into in traffic like a mad man. For as long as Eric had known, Kelly he had never spoke to her like that and now it was eating him up inside. Eric wasn't like the rest of the Mason family; Millie had raised him to be a gentleman and to have respect for women.

Just as Eric was about to get on the highway he noticed flashing lights in his rear view mirror. "Just great," he huffed as he pulled over to the side of the road. Eric removed his wallet from his back pocket and removed his driver's license. "What seems to be the problem officer?" Eric said with a smile. That smile was quickly wiped off his face when he was roughly snatched out the vehicle and tossed down to the grown. Eric's eyes grew wide in shock when he looked up and saw Mike standing over him with a nightstick in his hand. Before Eric got a chance to say a word, a black pillowcase was quickly placed over his head. "What the fuck is going on!" Eric yelled as he was picked up and violently tossed in the back of a van. While in the back of the van, Eric could hear Mike as well several other men's voices. When the van finally stopped, Eric was roughly snatched out the van and the pillowcase was removed from his head. When his blurred eyes focused, he saw Mike standing in front of him while several other officers surrounded him.

"What's this all about?" Eric asked with a scared look on his face. Without warning, Mike turned and slapped the taste out of Eric's mouth.

"You don't speak unless you're spoken too cocksucker!" Mike snarled. "This is a warning to you and the Mason family," Mike paused. "We're on the Mason family's ass make sure you let Derrick know that his days as a free man are numbered."

"Mike why are you doing..."

Mike spun and punched Eric in the pit of his stomach before he could finish his sentence, scared that he may have said something that he wasn't supposed to. Mike felt bad when he saw Eric double over in pain but he had to make it look believable to the rest of his fellow officers. Mike knew Eric wasn't built for lifestyle but unfortunately, for him he was associated by blood. He roughly snatched Eric up to his feet, "Tell the Mason family to watch their backs," Mike said as him and his fellow officers hopped back in the van. They dramatically let the tires spin as they pulled off blowing dirt back in Eric's face.

Eric stood in the middle of nowhere as tears rolled down his face. He never wanted to be a gangster or live this type of life, but it was forced on him by his family. As Eric headed down the dark street, he pulled out his cell phone and called the only person who understood him. The phone rung three times before a woman answered. "Hey mommy."

"What's wrong son, talk to me," Millie said. She could always tell when something was wrong with her favorite son.

"Can you talk for a minute?"

MIKE

9

Mike sat at the bar in Hooters sipping on a vodka and cranberry juice. Inside he felt bad about having to put his hands on Eric. He knew Eric was a good man and didn't deserve that, but he was just doing his job. Being a part of the Mason family and one of the city's best detective's was really beginning to put a strain on Mike and he wasn't sure how much longer he would be able to serve both sides. He knew soon that it was going to come to the point where he would have to choose a side.

"Wanna talk about it?"

Mike looked up and saw a beautiful Latin woman standing before him dressed in a silver dress looking like she had just stepped off of someone's red carpet. The Latin woman had perfect skin with light eyes, and hair that came down a little pass her shoulders not to mention her body was flawless. "Huh?"

The Latin woman sat down on the empty stool next to Mike and waved the bartender over. "Yeah let me get a bottle of mango Absolute, some orange juice, and two glasses," she said then turned her gaze on the man sitting next to her. "I said do you want to talk about it?"

Mike chuckled, "Is it that obvious?"

The Latin woman smiled and extended her hand. "Nicole Alvarez."

"Mike Brown," he shook Nicole's hand.

"Nice to meet you Mike." Nicole immediately poured two drinks and slid one over towards Mike.

"Likewise," Mike smiled as he sipped his drink. "Your last name is Alvarez. You wouldn't happen to be the daughter of Joey Alvarez?"

Nicole smiled. "Why are you scared of my father?"

"Not scared of anyone," Mike answered quickly. "But I'm no fool either." Mike had heard stories about the black men who tried to date Joey's

Alvarez's daughter and they all ended with their bodies never being found. "What are you doing in a place like this anyway?"

Nicole nodded up towards the several TV screens. "Here to watch this UFC fight."

Mike sipped his drink. "Yeah Ronda Rousey is a beast," he said as he felt his cell phone vibrating on his hip, he looked down and saw Derrick's name flashing across the screen. "It was nice talking to you but I have to get going," he stood up to leave when he felt Nicole reach out and grab his arm.

"I would like to take you out on a date some time if you're not too busy," Nicole smiled, devilishly licking her lips.

"I don't think that would be a good idea."

"Here's my card Mike if you change your mind give me a call," Nicole smiled as she watched, Mike make his exit.

Mike stepped out of the sports bar and quickly called Derrick back. "Hey pop."

"I saw you sent me a text that said "666" is everything alright?" Derrick asked.

"We have a problem," Mike began. "My boss has got a hard on for the Mason Family and is willing to do everything to bring us down."

"It's your job to not let that happen," Derrick said in a stern tone. "I mean that is why I pay you the big bucks am I right?"

"Absolutely but I just think maybe you should slow down a little until this heat dies down you know?"

"No I don't know," Derrick capped back. "Money doesn't sleep and neither do I."

"Pop they are coming down on the family weather you like it or not," Mike explained. "I'm not telling you what to do, but if I were you..."

"Well you're not!" Derrick cut him off. "Are you forgetting the rules son? It's the cop's job to catch me and it's my job not to get caught."

"Me and couple of my partners ran into Eric today and roughed him up," Mike said rubbing his hands over his waves. "If you speak to him tell him that I'm sorry, but I had to make it look believable."

"Don't worry about Eric he needs to toughen up anyway," Derrick laughed. "You just keep me posted on what's going on out here in these streets and don't forget that you too are a part of this family."

"I'll never forget that, I'm a Mason for life," Mike said proudly. He knew that things weren't going to play out well because Derrick didn't know how to back down. At the end of the day, he may not have been a Mason by blood, but he was connected to the Mason's through the money.

"Business is business."

"Business is business," Mike replied then ended the call.

DERRICK

10

"But pop why do I have to go to Florida?" Jimmy complained. He had sat there for over an hour listening to his father lecture him about him murdering the Ricardo brothers.

"You got us into this shit now you're going to get us out of it!" Derrick barked. "I've told you over and over again to start thinking before you react. You keep it up and soon we'll all be sitting in a cell because of you."

"Pop I keep telling you the Ricardo brothers left me no choice," Jimmy tried to explain. "And now it feels like we're working for the Alvarez family, he's got us doing hits for him for free at that," Jimmy huffed. "I would have rather gone to war then be someone's bitch."

"What did you just say?" Derrick asked getting up in Jimmy's face. "You just call me a bitch?"

"I didn't say that. What I said was I would rather go to war then be Alvarez's bitch," Jimmy stood his ground.

"You killed Joey Alvarez's hit men so now you have to go hit two men of his choosing," Derrick looked at Jimmy like he wanted to rip his son's head off. "You brought this all on yourself son, I can't keep on saving you."

"I don't need you to save me I can handle my own." Jimmy didn't like the fact that Derrick was willing to take orders from, Joey Alvarez. "I just don't believe you are making me do a hit for another man. A man you don't even care for at that," he paused. "If Millie was here we would be going to war right now."

"Well Millie ain't here right now and like I said you got us in this mess and now you have to get us out of this, nothing personal but business is business." Derrick said as he watched Jimmy make his exit.

MILLIE

11

Millie sat on her bunk skimming through the hip-hop weekly magazine that she held. She may have been in jail but she had to keep up with what was going on, on the outside. On the inside it was, Millie that supplied drugs to the entire population she basically ran the jail. Derrick couldn't believe how much money she was able to send home every month. With the correction officers on the payroll Millie was basically free to do as she pleased and she wasn't afraid to throw her weight around if need be. Millie reached under her pillow, grabbed her cell phone just as she got ready to send Derrick a text she heard a guard tap on her cell door with her nightstick.

"Mason you have a visitor here to see you," the C.O. announced. She waited patiently outside of the cell as, Millie got dressed. She made sure to take her time and make sure she looked right before leaving her cell. Fifteen minutes later, Millie stepped foot in the visiting room and spotted Eric sitting next to one of the vending machines. She walked over and gave Eric a warm motherly hug. "It's good to see you son."

"Hey mom sorry for just popping up on you like this," he apologized.

"I'm your mother you can come see me anytime and you don't have to have a reason to come see me," Millie placed her hand on top of Eric's hand and rubbed it gently. "Now tell momma what's wrong."

Eric let out a long breath. "I don't even know where to start," he shook his head. "I've been getting harassed and assaulted by the police a lot lately. I think something bad is going to happen soon and I'm getting scared."

"When you say something bad what do you mean?"

"The police have been on us real heavy lately I'm afraid that the whole family is going to be put in jail."

"Have you been keeping your nose clean like we've talked about?" Millie asked with a raised brow. She had sacrificed a lot to keep Eric on the right path and was willing to do whatever it took to protect, him. "You the one person in the family that has to be clean. If anything ever happens to this family, it's going to be your job to take care of all of us while we're in jail. You're the family security blanket and I need you to know that it's going to be your strength that saves this family one day."

"But what if you're wrong, what if I'm just a coward," Eric spoke freely. He didn't have the confidence to rush or save the family, all he cared were his investments and bringing in as much money as possible.

"Your mother don't spit out no cowards," Millie smiled. "Now tell me what's going on with these police."

"It's been crazy," Eric shook his head. "It's like the entire force is after our family and nobody else."

"What about, Mike? I know he's doing the best he can."

"He and a few of his buddy's pulled me other the other day and he really worked me over," Eric said looking down at the table. "I didn't tell dad because I knew all he was going to say was that I needed to man up."

"Let me tell you something son," Millie leaned forward. "Mike has rescued this family from many of situations and has always been true to this family if he laid his hands on that's because he must of had no choice. I raised that boy since he was one years old and I trust him," she paused. "All I need you focusing on is business nothing else."

"It's been a little hard to focus lately especially since me and Kelly have been fighting like cats and dogs."

"Hmmp," Millie huffed. She never liked or cared for Kelly since the first day Eric brought her home. It was just something about Kelly that just seemed to rub Millie the wrong way. "What's that girl's problem now?"

"I think she's cheating on me," Eric said with a sad look on his face. He couldn't prove it but all the signs were there. "She sneaks out the house and be going missing for hours."

Millie leaned forward. "You make sure you keep a close eye on that girl I never trusted her from day one and you know I'm never wrong about a person."

"Yeah I know," Eric pinched the bridge of his nose. "You think Kelly's cheating on me?"

"You'll be lucky if that's all she's doing," Millie said with a disgusted look on her face. "Do me a favor son can you get me an apple juice out of the vending machine?"

"Yeah of course," Eric stood up and headed over towards the vending machine, just as he was about to stick his dollar in the machine a muscular, rough faced man bumped into, him.

"Damn nigga watch where the fuck you going!" The big man growled.

"Sorry about that my brother I didn't see you," Eric apologized.

The big man's face crumbled up. "My brother?" He echoed. "I look like your brother to you motherfucker?"

Before Eric could say another word, he saw Millie approaching the big man from behind. He quickly moved out the way as Millie grabbed a chair and violently cracked it over the man's head.

"You over here fucking with my son!" Millie barked as she repeatedly stomped the big man's head into the floor before several officer tackled her down to the floor. "Get the fuck off me!" She yelled as the officers dragged her out of the visiting room kicking and screaming.

JIMMY

12

Jimmy sat in the passenger seat of the rented Benz with an aggravated look on his face. He still couldn't believe that Derrick was making him kill someone for Joey Alvarez. He and Big foot sat staked out front of the house of their intended target. They had been watching the house for the last two hours. Jimmy felt his phone vibrate on his hip; he looked down and saw that Kelly had sent him a few naked pictures of herself. He quickly replied back then put his phone away.

"I'm starving I need to get something to eat," Bigfoot said rubbing his stomach. He was tired of sitting in the car and needed to stretch his legs.

"Come on, I got an idea," Jimmy stepped out the Benz and headed for the back door of the house with Big foot close on his heels. They both slipped their hands in a pair of latex gloves. Big foot pulled out his silenced 9mm and shot the lock off the back door. Once Inside the house, Jimmy headed straight for the refrigerator.

"Fuck is you doing?" Bigfoot asked when he saw Jimmy pulled out some lunchmeat and cheese.

"Making us some sandwiches you said you were hungry right?" Jimmy smiled. He was the only person who was crazy enough to wear a three thousand dollar suit on a hit. According to him, he liked to do everything in style.

"Can you believe Derrick?" Jimmy took a bite from his sandwich. "If this was a few years ago we would be going to war with, Joey Alvarez over something like this."

"I guess he's just trying to keep the piece," Big foot shrugged. "Besides a war would definitely be bad for business."

"He's getting soft," Jimmy shoved the rest of his sandwich in his mouth. "I think it's time for me to take over the family business."

"You would probably run the business straight into the ground," Big foot teased as he heard keys jingling in the door. Jimmy quickly pulled his silenced 9mm from the small of his back and positioned himself behind a wall. When he heard footsteps and saw the light flick on, Jimmy sprang from behind the wall and fired off two shots. Pst, Pst!

Jimmy watched as the man that he had come to kill collapse face first down to the floor with a huge gaping hole in the center of his throat. He then trained his gun on the woman, and watched as a bullet from his gun exploded in the woman's face before she even got a second to scream. Jimmy looked down and saw two kids staring up at him with fear in their little eyes.

"Our work here is done come on let's get out of here," Big foot said, but stopped short when he noticed that Jimmy hadn't moved. "Don't even think about it," Big foot warned. He saw that look in, Jimmy's eyes a lot during the years of them working together so he already knew what was about to come next.

"They saw our faces," Jimmy whispered, then fired off two more bullets.

Pst, Pst!

Big foot looked down at the two children lying dead on the floor in a pool of their own blood and shook his head sadly. "You didn't have to do that."

"Business is business," Jimmy said, holstered his gun, and then headed back out the same door that he and Jimmy had broken into. Big foot took one last look at the children before following his partner back out the back door.

DERRICK

13

"Yeah baby right there," Derrick moan as he laid flat on his stomach. Pearl straddled his lower back, giving him a much-needed massage. Pearl was a good woman and planned on being with Derrick for the rest of her life. Derrick on the other hand loved Pearl but just wanted to have some fun with her until his wife was released from prison. He knew there was no way that Pearl would take the news well so he planned on easing it on her slowly.

"I heard about this new restaurant that's supposed to be awesome," Pearl smiled. "I was thinking maybe we could check it out, my treat."

"Sorry baby I can't. I have a few things that need my immediate attention," Derrick sat up. Word on the streets was that a few of Joey Alvarez's men had begun to move into Derrick's territory. He was going to check it out on his own; he just hoped and prayed that the rumors weren't true.

"Why does it seem like everything is more important than me?" Pearl huffed.

"Business is business," Derrick replied as he began getting dress. He hated how clingy Pearl was becoming and hoped that she got her act together before he had to cancel her.

"So one day of you hanging out with me and not doing any business is going to kill you?"

"Yup." Derrick said sarcastically.

"You're an asshole!" Pearl yelled and stormed upstairs. Seconds later, Derrick heard the bedroom door slam. He walked to the bathroom, glanced in the mirror, adjusted his tie, and walked from the bathroom to the living room where he saw his personal bodyguard Tony sitting on the couch flipping through the pages of a magazine.

"Let's go do this," Derrick said as he and Tony exited the house and slid in the back seat of the Maybach that awaited them. "So are you sure that it's Joey Alvarez's men that opened up in our territory?" He wanted to make sure, before he made a final decision.

Tony nodded his head. "A few of our men said that it was definitely Joey's men and they're not even trying to hide it."

The more Derrick listened the more it pissed him off. He couldn't believe that Joey would have the audacity to violate the code like that. Disrespect like this was like a slap in the face and something that Derrick had killed for, for less. For the rest of the ride he sipped on a drink as Anita Baker's voice hummed softly through the speakers.

Thirty minutes later the Maybach pulled up in front of a bodega. Derrick and Tony stepped out of the luxury car and approached two low level dealers that stood on the corning. "Do you two have permission to be on this corner?" Derrick asked.

"Who the fuck are you?" The man in the hoodie spat.

"If you two want to post up on this real estate then you're going to have to pay the owner," Derrick told them. He could tell just from looking at the two men that they had no clue how this territory thing worked.

"Check this out old head we got permission to be here," the one in the hoodie said in a matter of fact tone. "We work for Joey Alvarez," the man said proudly.

Without warning, Derrick pulled his .38 from his holster and shot the man with the hoodie in the face. His partner took off in a sprint but quickly dropped down to the concrete with two bullet holes in his back. "Fucking idiots!" Derrick growled as he and Tony hopped back in the Maybach. "Get Joey on the phone!"

ERIC

14

Eric sat at the dining room table alone eating a piece of pizza. Once again, Kelly had went missing and wasn't answering her phone. Now her disappearances were becoming more frequent and way more obvious. As Eric ate his pizza his mother's word kept replaying over in his head. "I never trusted her." Just the thought of his wife with another man angered Eric to the point where he wanted to inflict pain on someone even though that wasn't his thing. Eric emptied his plate in the trash when he heard the front door open then close. Seconds later, he heard the familiar sound of his wife's heels ringing loudly off the hard wood floor.

"And where have you been?" Eric asked as soon as he laid eyes on his wife.

"Not right now Eric," Kelly said as if he had ruined her entire day just by him asking a question.

"I've had a long day and my head is killing me," she said heading towards the stairs. Eric ran and stood in front of the stairs blocking Kelly's path.

"You're not going nowhere until you tell me where you the fuck you've been!" Eric yelled with fire dancing his eyes. "You've been gone for over six hours!"

"The last time I checked I was grown and didn't have a curfew!" Kelly capped back as she tried to step around Eric but he slid to the side still blocking her path.

"You ain't going nowhere until you tell me where you were!" Eric stood his ground.

"I hate you!" Kelly grown. "You treat me like a fucking child and you wonder why I hate being around you!" She cleared her throat and spat in Eric's face.

Eric wiped his face with his hand as he watched Kelly storm back out the front door. He thought about going after her but instead he decided to just let her go.

JOEY ALVAREZ

15

When Joey got word that Derrick had killed two men associated with his organization he made it his personal business to go meet with the head of the Mason Family. His limousine pulled up in front of the Mason estate. The driver held the door open as Joey stepped out and he was immediately met by Tony and another member of Derrick's security team.

"Right this way," Tony escorted Joey through the mansion. As Joey walked through the mansion, he noticed that Derrick Mason's security was airtight; several armed guards patrolled the mansion as if it was the White House.

Joey reached the bar area of the mansion and saw Derrick and Jimmy sitting a table having a drink. Joey helped himself to a seat not waiting for an invite. "Have you lost your mind?"

Derrick smiled and sipped his drink. "What seems to be the problem?"

"You murdered two of my men and you think this is funny?" Joey asked with a mean scowl on his face.

"Your men were in territory that they shouldn't have been in," Derrick shrugged. "My territory, my rules."

"You still owe me!" Joey growled. "My men were there to help pay off the debt that you owe."

"That's not what we agreed on," Derrick snapped. "The agreement was one million dollars and I do two favors for you. I never agreed for your men to come on to my territory and get rid of product."

"That retard son of yours killed two made men!" Joey snapped. "You're in position to negotiate and besides you still owe me a favor."

"Fuck you, our deal is off!" Jimmy said speaking for the first time. Derrick went to say something but Jimmy continued. "Those made men of yours were in one of our properties being disrespectful and got what they deserved."

"You arrogant fool you don't even know the type of shit you just got your entire family in," Joey stood to his feet with a smirk on his face. "This is just why I hate working with you niggers."

"Fuck you just said?" Jimmy hopped to his feet. Derrick tried to grab him but it was too late, Jimmy was already in motion. Jimmy snuffed Joey and watched the old man dramatically crash down to the floor. "Fuck you think you talking to like that?" Jimmy barked as he violently stomped Joey's head into the floor repeatedly. "Motherfucker!"

Derrick slowly stood to his feet and walked over to his son. "Do you know what you just did?"

"Fuck him. I'm not sitting back letting him disrespect the entire family," Jimmy huffed. "What's gotten into you lately? If this was back in the day you would have been put a clown like this six feet under."

Derrick gave Jimmy a sad look. "Son this is not back in the day and you can't go around killing made men and you especially can't go around killing the boss of a made family. At this level there are rules son and you just put us in a real bad place."

"I'm not just gon sit back and let a clown like him disrespect us."

"That's why I'm the boss of this family because if you were in control there wouldn't be no family, because you would have been got us all murdered," Derrick explained but he could see that Jimmy still didn't get it.

Tony stepped in the room and stopped mid-stride when he saw Joey Alvarez laid out on the floor. "What the fuck did you just do?" He asked looking at Jimmy with serious look on his face.

"What the fuck is the big deal?" Jimmy said with a confused look on his face. "Why is everybody scared of this old fuck?"

"You just gave all the big bosses the green light to wipe out this entire family," Tony shook his head. "You can't kill two made men then beat up a boss and live to tell about it."

Joey stirred and sat up on his elbows and spat out blood. "You all are dead men!"

Derrick pulled his .38 from his holster and aimed it at Joey's head.

"Wait you don't have to do this," Joey pleaded. "If you let me go I'll forget all about this."

Derrick looked Joey in the eyes and pulled the trigger. Jimmy and Tony watched Joey's head violently jerk back. Derrick looked over at Jimmy. "Make sure his body is never found and keep your mouth shut," he turned to Tony. "Make sure everyone in the family doesn't leave the house from now on without a gun and let them know to be on point at all times because there's a good chance that we'll wind up having to go to war with all the big bosses if word somehow gets out." He turned and faced Jimmy. "If you ever fuck up this bad again or do anything stupid to put this family at risk I promise you I will kill you myself."

MIKE

16

Mike sat in the hotel room rubbing Nicole Alvarez's back as she cried her eyes out. She called Mike in the middle of the night telling him that her father was missing and nobody had seen or heard from him in over ten days, which was weird. For the past three months, Mike and Nicole had been seeing each other almost every day, he knew by her being the daughter of Joey Alvarez made her forbidden, but the strong connection the two had proved to be easier said than done. "Stop crying baby I promise I'm going to do everything in my power to find your father."

Nicole wiped her eyes. "There's nothing you can do baby."

"I'm a cop I can use my resources and find him," Mike lied. Derrick had called a family meeting and explained to the family what exactly took place, warning everyone to be on point at all times.

"Last I heard my father was supposed to be meeting up with some arrogant asshole called Derrick Mason," Nicole paused to wipe her eyes. "My dad's big bosses are on their way up here now to speak to this Derrick guy. The whole family believes that Derrick Mason murdered my father but there's no proof yet, but trust me if there's any dirt the big bosses will find it."

"Why do they think that?"

"Family business stuff baby," Nicole said. "I've hired several investigators and I also have a few search parties out looking for my dad, hopefully we can get to the bottom of this and I just hope and pray that Derrick Mason has nothing to do with this because if so he and his entire family is going to suffer greatly."

"Just be patient baby and I promise you this is all going to work itself out," Mike said nervously. He could already see this situation spiraling out of control and it was up to him to somehow get the heat off the Mason Family and to protect them. Mike grabbed both sides of Nicole's face with his hands and kissed her passionately. "Let's go get something to eat baby."

Mike and Nicole exited the hotel room hand in hand. Mike hated that he had to be in the middle of a sticky situation like this. No matter what he did, it just seemed like his life always turned out messy. Mike reached Nicole's Range Rover when he heard footsteps coming from behind; he spun around and saw two mask men creeping up on him. "Get down!" Mike yelled as he grabbed Nicole and rushed her down to the ground just as the sound of machine gun fire woke up the streets. Bullets pinged loudly off the side of the Range Rover as shattered glass rained down on Mike and Nicole's head. Mike pulled his gun from his holster as the gunfire continued. Mike got ready to spring from behind the Range Rover when all of a sudden; the gunfire stopped and the sound of footsteps running in the opposite direction could be heard. He peek his head up and found that the mask men were gone. He looked down and saw a shaken up, Nicole crying her hysterically with a frightened look on her face. "I think the same people that killed my father are out to kill me," she trembled with each word spoken.

"Don't worry baby I'm not going to let that happen."

JIMMY

17

"What the fuck was Mike doing with that bitch?" Jimmy growled. He was on a mission to one by one take out the entire Alvarez family before they took out him and his family. But he had to move quietly so Derrick wouldn't find out what he was up to. In Jimmy's eyes, his father had turned soft and could no longer make the ugly decisions that a boss was required to make in this business. If Derrick knew that Jimmy was trying to kill Joey Alvarez's daughter it was no doubt in his mind that Derrick would have him murdered immediately.

"I think Mike is sleeping with Joey Alvarez's daughter," Big foot said. He too was caught off guard when he saw Mike and Nicole together. He and Jimmy could have easily killed Nicole but they backed off because of Mike.

"He just fucked everything up!" Jimmy barked, "Now she's more than likely going to have security detail around her twenty four hours a day." Jimmy wasn't just going to sit around and wait for them to come and kill him, if he had to go he planned on taking a lot more people with him. "We'll keep a close eye on her and take her out another day."

Big foot nodded. He knew what they were doing was wrong but he felt obligated to help Jimmy. "What now?"

"Calling it a night," Jimmy said as he pulled out his phone and texted Kelly. "Baby I need to see you tonight and wear something sexy." He wrote.

Big foot pulled up in front of Jimmy's house and placed the gear in park. "I'll be close by so if you need me just hit my jack," he held out his fist.

"No doubt," Jimmy bumped fist with Big foot. "And don't forget to get rid of those guns."

"I got you," Big foot said. He made sure that Jimmy was inside safely before he pulled off.

DERRICK

18

Derrick sat in the bar section of his home with a sad look on his face. He was expecting to meet with one of the big bosses tonight and to say he was nervous was an understatement. Everyone had been making a big deal about Joey Alvarez going missing and all signs were pointing to the Mason Family. The consequences for killing a boss was death. Death didn't scare Derrick. What scared Derrick was them killing his entire family. Derrick downed his drink in one gulp and quickly poured himself another as he noticed Tony and another guy from his security escort, Chico in his direction. Chico was one of the big bosses out in Columbia that didn't take no shit. Chico had an army of killers ready to go at a drop of a hat. Chico walked up in his expensive suit and held out his hand, "Derrick."

"Chico," Derrick shook his hand. "Sorry that you had to come all the way from Columbia for something like this."

"Tell me a little bit about the meeting that you and Joey had," Chico leaned back in his chair and crossed his legs.

"Well me and Joey had a meeting about me killing two men affiliated with his organization," Derrick said. "They were selling product in my territory without permission."

"I hear that your son killed two made men is this true?" Chico asked.

"Yes that is true."

"The consequences for an act like that is death you do know that right?"

Derrick nodded. "Yes I know."

"Joey Alvarez was last seen alive with you," Chico said with a raised brow. "So until his body turns up all fingers point to you for being responsible for his disappearance."

"That's ridiculous," Derrick sipped his drink. "We are all in the drug business which means we all have multiple enemies that would love to see us dead."

"That may be true but Joey Alvarez was last seen alive entering your home and if I find out that you or anyone in your family had anything to do with Joey's death I'm going to have you and your entire family killed," he said with a serious look on his face. "Also until this issue is resolved I will no longer be able to supply you or your family with product."

"What does you supplying us have to do with anything?" Derrick asked with a frown on his face.

"It has to do with everything," Chico said in a calm tone. "You are now officially under investigation and I pray that we don't find out that you had anything to do with the disappearance of Joey because I promise you it will not be good for you and your family."

"I'm not going to sit back and keep letting you threaten my family."

Chico smirked. "Mr. Mason I don't make threats."

Before, Derrick could say another word, Tony ran into the bar area with a nervous look on his face. "The cops are here and they have warrants!"

Derrick looked up and saw several detective's walking in his direction.

"Derrick Mason?" The lead detective called out. "You're under arrest for the murder of Casey Smith and Devon Alexander."

"I don't even know those men you just named," Derrick said, as he was being hand cuffed.

"That's strange because you killed both of them in front of a bodega not too long ago," the detective smiled.

"I didn't kill anyone."

"We have an eye witness that's identifying you as the shooter," the detective said proudly as they escorted Derrick out of his home and into the back of an unmarked car.

ERIC

19

Eric laid on the couch faking as if he was asleep. He was tired of Kelly sneaking out of the house refusing to tell him where she was going. While pretending to be sleep he could hear Kelly moving around the house getting dress. He heard the shower cut off then the smell of her perfume filled the air something that always happened before she would disappear. Minutes later he heard the front door open then close. Eric quickly jumped out and strapped on the bullet proof vest that his father had given him along with the 9mm the entire family was given to keep with them at all times for protection. Eric ran out the front door, hopped in his Benz, and took off behind Kelly. He made sure to stay at least five to six cars behind not wanting to give up his position and be spotted. Murderous thoughts filled Eric's mind as he cruised down the highway. Never in a million year would he have ever thought that he would one day have to tail his wife to find out what she was hiding from him. After a thirty-minute drive, Eric watched as Kelly pulled into Jimmy's driveway. "What the fuck?" He said out loud, as he watched Kelly step out of her car looking like a streetwalker. She wore a skimpy skirt that left little to the imagination.

"No way," Eric shook his head there was no way that this could be happening to him. Could his wife really be having an affair with his brother? Eric's mind was telling him no but his eyes were showing him something different. He grabbed the 9mm from off the passenger seat and studied it for a second. In all of his years living, Eric had never shot a gun before but for some reason he felt like tonight all that was going to change. Eric stepped out of his Benz and slowly made his way towards the front of his brother's house with the gun in his hand hanging freely down by his side. He walked up to the front door and placed his ear to it.

JIMMY

20

"**D**amn it's about time you got here," Jimmy sat on the couch with his legs spread apart stroking himself. He hated to admit it but he was beginning to fall in love with Kelly he knew it wasn't right but he couldn't help himself. Kelly was everything in a woman that he was looking for.

"Sorry baby I had to make sure that Eric was asleep first before I left," Kelly said as she easily slipped out of her dress and stood before Jimmy in her birthday suit.

Jimmy smiled as he stood to his feet. "Look what you did," he said nodding down to the erection that he held in his hand.

"I'm sorry daddy let me fix that for you," Kelly said in a sexy tone as she melted down to her knees and slowly slid her mouth up and down Jimmy's pole.

Jimmy grabbed a hand full of Kelly's blonde hair as he moved her head at a speed of his liking. "Aww yes baby suck that shit like a pacifier," he coached. "Mmmm that's what I'm talking about." Jimmy was just about to say some real freaky shit when he heard what sounded like a gunshot then saw his front door come busting open. Jimmy got ready to dash for his gun but stopped when he saw who had entered his home. "Fuck you doing here?"

Eric walked through the front door and saw his wife down on her knees orally pleasing his brother. The pain and hurt that he felt made him want to cry but he promised himself that he would stay strong. "So this is where you've been running off to I see."

"Eric what are you doing here!" Kelly yelled pissed off that she had been caught. "How did you find me?"

"I trusted you," Eric said in a light whisper. "I trusted you bitch!"

"You followed me?" Kelly asked with her face crumbled up. "How dare you follow me?" She walked up and slapped Eric across the face as if he was the one that had just got caught cheating.

Eric rubbed the side of his face, then without warning, he turned and hit Kelly over the top of her head with his gun. He was so mad that he could kill her right now.

"Fuck is you doing?" Jimmy's voice boomed snapping Eric out of his trance. "Don't come up in my house putting ya hands on my girl."

"Your girl?" Eric echoed. "That's my wife!" He said through clenched teeth. "My wife not yours!"

Jimmy smiled. "Shut ya bitch ass up you can't handle a woman like that, every night she complains to me how miserable she is with you."

"You shut your fucking mouth right now!" Eric yelled. "Or else!"

"Or else what motherfucker?" Jimmy said aggressively as he began walking towards his little brother. "Fuck you gon do with that gun?"

"You ruined my life!" Eric growled. "If it's one thing you don't do its mess with another man's wife." He said as he raised his arm, aiming his gun at Jimmy.

Jimmy stood there with a calm look on his face. "All I'm going to tell you is you better not miss," he told him. "You know the rules it never personal it's always business."

"Fuck business this is personal!" Eric growled then pulled the trigger.

POW!

DERRICK

21

"Mason!" The correction officer yelled. "You've made bail," he announced as he cracked the gate and escorted Derrick down to the intake area. At the front desk, waiting for Derrick was his lawyer, Mr. Goldberg.

"Before we go I just want to let you know that there are about a hundred cameras and reporters out there waiting for you," Mr. Goldberg said. "You say nothing just walk out and get in the back of the truck that awaits you."

Derrick nodded as he followed his lawyer out of the jail. Immediately, Mr. Goldberg and Derrick were swarmed by reporters.

"Derrick did you really murder those two men in cold blood?" A dark skin reporter asked shoving her phone close to his mouth.

"Is it true that there's a million dollar bounty on your head?" Another reporter asked.

"Derrick who tailor your suits?" A Chinese reporter asked.

Derrick kept quiet as his security pushed a hole through the crowd. Once Derrick and Mr. Goldberg were in the back seat of the Cadillac truck, it quickly pulled away from the curb. "What we looking like?" Derrick asked as he grabbed a glass and poured himself a much-needed drink.

"Not too good the detectives are claiming to have an eye witness, but if I grease the right palms it shouldn't be too hard to get a name," Mr. Goldberg said. "The bigger problem is there are several personal investigators out trying to find out anything they can about Joey Alvarez disappearing," he said in a serious tone. "Do not; I repeat do not talk on the phone unless you have to any business needs to be discussed face to face from now on."

Just by listening to his lawyer, Derrick knew he couldn't take this situation lightly. It felt as if the walls around him were all closing in on him at the same time. "I need the name of that eye witness."

"Working on that as we speak," Mr. Goldberg sent off a few text messages. "Also I think you should know that Jimmy was shot two days ago."

"Shot?" Derrick repeated. "I go to jail for forty eight hours and everything falls apart," he shook his head. "Who shot him and more importantly is he still alive?"

"He's still alive, but the cops are on him like flies on shit," Mr. Goldberg explained. "Me being your attorney and advisor I think maybe you should lay low for a while. Not only are the big bosses on your ass, but the cops are involved now too."

"In my line of work there's no such thing as laying low." Being the leader of a successful family came with a lot of tough choices and big decisions to make, and when things got rough you don't lay low you go even harder, it's the boss job to set an example and let everyone know just why they are the boss.

The big iron gate opened as the Cadillac truck pulled onto the Mason estate. The driver held the back door open as Derrick stepped out headed towards the front door, he stepped foot in the mansion and spotted Mike and Eric sitting at the bar area. "You two made up yet?"

"Eric still won't talk to me," Mike answered.

"You two are brothers shake hands and make up," Derrick ordered. With all the enemies that they had on the outside, it was no room for fighting amongst the family.

Mike and Eric reluctantly shook hands, whatever problems they had they would have to handle it at another time.

"The Columbians cut off our supply until further notice," Derrick began. "They are looking for any reason to pin the Joey Alvarez murder on me and destroy our entire family."

"So without supply how will we stay afloat?" Mike asked.

"Eric here has made some wonderful investments for this family so money is not and never will be a problem," Derrick said proudly. "Are loan shark business is booming right now as well the four gambling spots we have, but in order to keep our territory we are going to need product," he said looking over at Mike.

Mike nodded his head. "I'll shake down as many dealers as possible and get us as much product as I can."

"Also, Jimmy is in the hospital somebody shot him," Derrick announced. "I think the Columbians may have hired a secret hit squad to take us out one by one so make sure you all..."

"Wasn't no hit squad that shot Jimmy it was me," Eric said surprising everyone in the room.

Derrick laughed loudly. "That was a good one son don't joke like that."

"Jimmy was sleeping with my wife so I shot him," Eric said with a stone look on his face. Just the thought of it made Eric angry all over again.

Derrick got up in Eric's face. "So you're telling me you shot your brother over some slut?"

"She's not a slut she's my wife."

"I don't give a fuck whose wife she is!" Derrick grabbed Eric and forcefully shoved his back into the wall. "You don't go against your family for no one I don't care who it is especially not some fucking outsider!"

"You don't sleep with a man's wife pop that's an unspoken rule," Eric said. "Jimmy knew exactly what he was doing."

"I know Jimmy may not have been the greatest brother to you growing up, but he's still family and family is all we got right now," Derrick explained. He knew that if the family had to go to war they would have to stick together to even stand a bit of a chance.

"I'm sorry pop I should have come to you first," Eric admitted.

Derrick pulled Eric in for a hug. "It's going to be okay. I'll talk to Jimmy and fix this, go home and get you some rest while I talk to Mike about a few things."

Mike waited until Eric made his exit before he spoke. "Make sure you keep an eye on him you know Jimmy's not going to be too happy when he gets out of the hospital and you know how his temper is."

"Jimmy got what he deserved," Derrick spat as he poured himself a drink and downed it in one gulp. It was Jimmy's fault why the family was in the bind they were in at this very moment. "Jimmy's got a lot of growing up to do so maybe him getting shot will help with that."

Mike looked down at his phone and saw that he had a text message from Nicole. "Hey baby when you get a chance come see me I got some news on the Mason Family. I told you they were no good." Mike read the text message and slipped his phone back down into his pocket. "I gotta get out of here pops I'll call you later," Mike hugged, Derrick and quickly made his exit.

KELLY

22

After spending two days in the hospital sitting by Jimmy's bed, Kelly decided to head home so she could take a shower and change clothes. She still couldn't believe that Eric had really shot Jimmy. Kelly never saw that one coming. A part of her felt bad about cheating on Eric and him having to find out like that, but the other part of her said fuck him and his feelings. Kelly looked at her reflection in the rear view mirror and cringed at the bandage on the side of her head from where Eric had hit her with his gun. "I should have snitched on his ass," Kelly said out loud. The last thing she was expecting was for Eric to strike her. Kelly pulled into the driveway of her and Eric's house and killed the engine. She stepped out her Range Rover in her skimpy skirt and some flip flops on her feet. Kelly walked through the front door and noticed all of her things neatly packed and placed by the door.

Seconds later, Eric appeared downstairs wearing a pair of black slacks and a wife beater, holding a bottle of Grey Goose in his hand. "Fuck is you doing here?"

"I live here," Kelly said as she noticed the gun sticking out of Eric's waistband.

"Not no more you don't," Eric took a swig from his bottle. "You wanna go run the streets and be a hoe."

"I made a mistake, Eric."

"Fucking my brother is not a mistake," Eric countered. He didn't even want to see Kelly let alone talk about her cheating and lying ways all it was going to do was piss him off even further.

"Eric I know you're mad at me but I'm still you're wife and I'm not going anywhere this is our home," Kelly said forcing out some fake tears. After giving it a lot of thought, Kelly realized she had a really good man she just hoped that it wasn't too late to repair their marriage.

Eric looked at, Kelly as if she was crazy. "You ain't my wife and you ain't staying under the same roof as me ever again!" He barked. "I'll kill you before I let that happen!"

"What's gotten into you, Eric?" Kelly said with a confused look on her face. "You're drinking, carrying guns when did all this start?"

"I don't really have too much to live for right now," Eric shrugged. "My wife is out fucking my brother and more than likely Jimmy is going to kill me when he's released from the hospital I might as well enjoy my last few days that I have left on this earth," he turned his bottle up.

"We have to work this out baby," Kelly said as tears rolled down her face. "You have to forgive me you're all I got."

"You got Jimmy now," Eric chuckled. He knew his brother ran through women as if he did draws and could only imagine all the foul shit he was going to put Kelly through.

"I don't want Jimmy. I want you."

"I want you out of here," he said in a calm tone.

"I don't have to go anywhere this is my house too," Kelly said folding her arms across her chest standing her ground.

Eric pulled the gun from his waistband and aimed it at, Kelly's chest. "I'm going to count to five," he said in a calm tone. "One...Two...Three..."

"Fuck you. Eric. You'll be hearing from me and my lawyer real soon!" Kelly yelled as she left and slammed the door behind her.

NICOLE ALVAREZ

23

Nicole laid across the king sized bed her hotel suit naked reading an article about Derrick Mason on her iPhone. She hated Derrick with a passion and couldn't wait to hear the great news of him getting his head blown off. Nicole tossed her phone on the bed when she heard a knock at the door. She looked through the peephole and smiled when she saw Mike standing on the other side of the door. "Hey baby," she stepped to the side so Mike could enter.

"Hey baby," Mike kissed Nicole on the lips. "I got here as fast as I could." He was interested to hear what she had to tell him about Derrick.

"Remember how I was telling you that the Mason Family were a bunch of violent animals?"

Mike nodded. "Yeah I remember."

"Well I heard that Derrick's son, Jimmy Mason killed two of my father's men and when my father went to confront Derrick Mason about it and that's when that animal murdered my father," Nicole said as if she saw all this happen with her own eyes.

"Do you have proof or evidence that, that's the way it went down?" Mike asked. He knew her story was bullshit but he couldn't just come out and say it.

"Yes a friend of the family told me that's how it went down."

"So now what?"

"I hired these two hit men to take that animal Derrick Mason out of his misery," Nicole said with fire dancing in her eyes. If she had to she was willing to pay a fortune to get rid of Derrick Mason.

"You shouldn't be telling me this knowing that I'm a cop," Mike pointed out.

"Derrick Mason is going to get murdered regardless if I make it happen or not it's only a matter of time before the big bosses figure this out," Nicole shrugged. "I figured why wait for the inevitable."

"What happens if Derrick Mason survives the hit then what?"

Nicole smiled. "Trust me they won't. I hired the Lopez twins."

Eddie Lopez and Danny Lopez were two well-known hit men that took care of problems in the underworld. They were known for killing their victims in cold blood. They were usually hired when someone wanted to send a message. On every one of the Lopez twins hits there were over two hundred shell casings found when it was all said and done. Mike knew exactly who the Lopez Twins were and what they were capable of.

"Damn you must really believe Derrick Mason was behind your father's disappearance," Mike said as he began to formulate a plan to stop the hit from going down. There was no way he was going to sit around and let the Lopez Twins murder the man that raised him since he was a child.

"Trust me Mike, Derrick murdered my father," she said in a matter of fact tone.

Mike stood to his feet. "I have to get going baby you just make sure you be careful these men sound very dangerous."

Nicole laid back on the bed and spread her legs open exposing her freshly waxed pussy. "I know you don't think you're leaving without taking care of her," she said with a devilish grin on her face.

Mike smiled as he slid down onto the bed and slowly tongue kissed Nicole's fat pussy lips. Mike took his time and slowly licked and sucked on her magic button. Nicole bucked her hips as she grabbed the back of Mike's head forcing his face even further into her wetness.

"Yes...yes... yes!" Nicole moaned, the louder, Mike slurped the more it turned her on.

Mike shook his head from side to side, as he felt, Nicole's body start to shake.

"Hmmm!" She moaned as she reached her climax.

Mike smiled as he watched, Nicole forcefully push him down on the bed and climb on top of him. "Whatever plans you had you better cancel them because I'm about to tear you up!" She said through clenched teeth.

JIMMY

24

Jimmy stepped foot in his father's mansion with a scowl on his face and his arm in a sling. He was still beyond pissed that he had been shot by his little brother and he couldn't wait to bump into Eric face-to-face. Close on Jimmy's heels was Big foot. He too was upset that Eric had shot Jimmy. He knew if he were there, it would have been a different story.

Derrick sat in the den sipping on a drink when he noticed Jimmy and Big foot enter. "Have a seat," he ordered. Derrick finished off his drink then looked up at Jimmy. "What happen between you and Eric?"

"I'm going to kill him when I see him end of story," Jimmy said simply. There was no way he was going to let anyone get away with shooting him, blood or not.

"You were fucking the man's wife correct? Then what did you expect him to do?"

"He didn't have to shoot me," Jimmy huffed.

"If you were fucking my wife I would have shot you too," Derrick said seriously. He knew, Jimmy was pissed off but he had to somehow defuse the situation before his sons tried to kill one another. "Listen your brother is on the way I want you two to talk this out and make it right."

"I have a hole in my shoulder ain't nothing to talk about." Jimmy snapped.

"There's a lot going on right now and the last thing I need are my sons trying to kill each other!" Derrick's voice boomed. "Eric is on his way over, you're going to apologize for fucking his wife, and the two of you are going to go back to being brothers! Do you understand me?"

Jimmy nodded. "Yeah pop I understand." Jimmy was already in hot water with his old man so he decided to keep quiet for now, but when the time presented itself, he planned on returning the favor.

Twenty minutes later, Eric stepped in the den in a black, slim fitting tailored suit. Immediately, Derrick could tell that Eric was wearing a bulletproof vest or some kind of chest protector underneath his suit. Derrick's eyes then eased their way down to Eric's waist where he saw a bulge, which told him that Eric was strapped. A smile quickly appeared on his face he had never seen Eric like this before. Derrick knew that catching Jimmy having sex with his wife had pushed Eric over the top and maybe just maybe it was for the better. "Hey pop," Eric nodded then turned and faced Jimmy. "Jimmy." He greeted.

Jimmy said nothing.

"You two are brothers and it won't be no fighting amongst the family so you two better figure out a way to make up," Derrick said. "Now if you'll excuse me, Mike has been calling me off the hook I have to call him back," he said then disappeared out of the den. Big foot followed, Derrick's lead, and stepped out leaving the two brothers alone so they could talk.

Once the two were alone, Jimmy stood to his feet and looked Eric in his eyes. "This shit ain't over. I'm going to make you pay for what you did."

"I apologize I shouldn't of shot you. I lost my cool," Eric said in a calm tone. "Blood is thicker than water and I just pray that one day you forgive me and we can go back to being brothers."

"Fuck you!" Jimmy snapped. "Once my shoulder heals I'm coming for you and I pray to God that you're ready."

Eric nodded. "I'll be well prepared for whatever it is that comes my way." He knew there was no way that Jimmy could forgive him for shooting him that's just not how Jimmy operated. Violence was Jimmy's game and he had the guts, and heart to do all the things other men didn't. Just as Eric was about to reply both men noticed Derrick re-enter the room with a mean scowl on his face.

"What's wrong pop?" Eric asked sensing that something wasn't right.

"Just got off the phone with Mike," Derrick paused for a second. "Joey Alvarez's daughter just hired the Lopez Twins to take me out."

"Damn!" Jimmy huffed. The Lopez Twins were legends in his eyes. They were as violent as they came and would do whatever it took to get the job done. "Beef up your security and I'll see if I can find the Lopez Twins and maybe have a word with them."

"Ain't no talking to the Lopez Twins once they've accepted a contract that's it," Derrick said. "We're going to handle business as usual this isn't the first time I've had a hit put on me and it probably won't be the last."

"I don't think this is something that you should be taking lightly," Eric said. He didn't know much about how things worked in the family business, but even he knew who the Lopez Twins were. "Beef up your security you're the head of this family and we need you here."

Derrick looked over at Eric and smiled he liked the way his son was thinking. "I may need you to go pick up some cash for me."

"Who me?" Eric said with a surprised look on his face.

"Yeah you."

"I don't think that would be a good idea. Mom said she wanted my hands to always stay clean," Eric said with a nervous look on his face.

"Usually that's Jimmy's job but since you shot him he's not able to do his job now you have to take on his responsibilities until he's back healthy," Derrick told him. "Think you can handle that?"

Eric nodded. "Sure pop no problem."

Derrick turned and looked at Jimmy and Big foot. "While he's doing that I need you two to find out where Joey Alvarez's daughter is hiding at."

"My pleasure," Jimmy said. He was mad at himself for letting Nicole Alvarez get away the other night if he had killed her when he had the chance then there wouldn't be a contract on his father's head right now. "We may have a small problem pop," Jimmy said. "I think Joey Alvarez's daughter is Mike's new sweetheart."

"This isn't up for discussion!" Derrick snapped. "I don't care about no sweetheart find her and let me know when you do!"

MIKE

25

Mike sat behind the wheel of his vehicle as he watched the Lopez Twins exit the airport. Just from looking at the two men, he could tell that they meant business and didn't fly all the way to New York to fuck around. "What the hell?" Mike said to himself as he leaned forward and noticed the two brother got into separate cabs. Having to make a quick decision, Mike decided to follow Eddie Lopez. He would have to catch, Danny Lopez another time. Mike pulled out behind Eddie Lopez's cab. He had no idea what the Lopez Twins had up their sleeves, but he planned on finding out.

Mike followed the cab into Queens; he had been following the cab for thirty minutes and finally decided enough was enough. The cab turn on a quiet street and Mike immediately hit his lights signaling for the cab to pull over. Mike reached under his seat and grabbed the .380 with the serial numbers scratched off; he quickly screwed a silencer on the barrel and stepped out the car. Mike walked up to the driver's window and leaned down. "Where you guys headed?"

"Just dropping off a passenger; why am I being pulled over?" The cab driver asked. Without warning, Mike raised his arm and shot the cab driver in his face at point blank range. He then moved toward the back seat and unloaded the rest of his clip into Eddie Lopez's body. Mike quickly jogged back to his car and pulled off in a hurry. One of the Lopez Twins were eliminated. Now Mike had to find Danny Lopez before he made it to Derrick. Mike drove down the street and prayed that no one had seen the deadly act he just committed, cause not only would he lose his job he would also lose his freedom. Mike was playing a deadly game and he knew it, but it was no way he was going to just sit around and let anyone take shots at his family. Mike grabbed his phone and dialed Derrick's number. After the third ring, Derrick answered. "Yeah."

"One brother down working on the next one," Mike said then hung up. He then dialed Nicole Alvarez's number. "Hey baby I need to see you. Where are you?"

ERIC

26

Eric walked through the hotel with one of his father's bodyguards close on his heels. This was his first time handling something illegal for his father and to say he was beyond nervous was an understatement. His job was simple; meet with a few men that owed the family some money and collect it. A simple in and out transaction. The only problem was word got out that Derrick Mason was now on borrowed time so a few business associates decided to try their hand and not pay what they owed. Usually, Jimmy handled these family problems but since, Jimmy was out of commission for a while, Eric had to step up to the plate.

Eric and the bodyguard stepped on the elevator and pressed seven. "Do me a favor, when we get back remind me to set up a meeting with the owner of this hotel." The hotel was beautiful and Eric thought it would be a good idea to invest in it. The two men stepped off the elevator and made their way down the hall until they found the door they were looking for.

"Step back sir," the bodyguard said as he raised his fist and knocked on the door. Seconds later a black man with baggy clothes answered the door.

"Come in, come in," he said then quickly closed the door.

Eric stepped in the room and instantly the smell of weed attacked his nose. He looked and counted three men in total.

"Where's Jimmy?" the man with baggy clothes ask as he took two quick drags from the blunt that he held between his lips.

"Jimmy sent me," Eric said firmly. "I was told you have something for me."

"You in a rush or something?"

"Actually I am," Eric answered. Something wasn't right but he couldn't pin point what it was. All three of the men looked sneaky like in any second they were going to put a bullet in his head.

"Introduce yourself bro," the man in the baggy clothes said. "I like to know who I'm doing business with."

"Derrick Mason sent me here to collect $80,000 do you have it or not?" Eric snapped he was tired of fucking around.

"Take it easy bro," the man in the baggy clothes smiled as he reached under the bed and tossed Eric a book bag. Eric took the book bag opened it and began to count the money.

"Damn it's all there you what you don't trust me or something?"

"Trust has nothing to do with this I don't know you," Eric said in a calm tone. He had heard a million times how dirty this business could be and didn't plan on taking any chances. Twenty minutes later, Eric counted $65,000. "There's $15,000 missing."

"You sure?" The man in the baggy clothes asked. "Nah its $80,000 in that bag I counted it myself."

"There's $15,000 missing," Eric repeated.

"Count it again," the man in the baggy clothes insisted. "I know for a fact there's $80,000 in that bag."

Eric sighed loudly as he pulled his 9mm from the holster on his waist and shot the man in the baggy clothes in the leg. He then quickly raised his gun at his two partners keeping them at bay.

"Son of a bitch you shot me!" The man in the baggy clothes growled.

Eric's bodyguard pulled out his gun and forced the other two men to the floor and held them there at gunpoint.

Eric aimed his gun at the man in the baggy clothes head. "Where's the rest of the money?"

"Under the bed just please don't kill me," he cried as he watched Eric reach under the bed and remove a small book bag. Eric stood there and counted every last dollar until the count was correct. He then walked over to the man in the baggy clothes, raised his foot and stomped the man's head into the floor. "From now on you and your crew will pay double for product do you understand me?"

The man in the baggy clothes nodded his head. "Yes I understand now can you please call me an ambulance?"

"Fuck you!" Eric said as him and his bodyguard exited the hotel room leaving the man lying in a pool of his own blood.

DERRICK

27

A four-man security crew escorted Derrick to the venue of a charity event that one of his companies was hosting. Derrick had no clue what the event was for all he knew was Eric was responsible for putting it together and it would look good for him to show his face for a while. Derrick laughed, sipped wine, and shook hands with the entire upper class guest that attended the function. Derrick was having a good time until he saw Pearl walk through the front door.

Pearl walked through the door dressed in a tight fitting white dress that clung to her voluptuous body. She had the body shape of a stripper and carried her goodies well. She spotted Derrick and immediately headed his way. "Hey baby," Pearl smiled with her arms open wide for a hug.

"Fuck are you doing here?" Derrick growled as he grabbed Pearl by the arm and escorted her over in the corner so everyone wouldn't be in there business. "You can't just be popping up on me like that."

"Well if you answered the phone when I called you then we wouldn't have this problem," Pearl folded her arms across her chest with an attitude. "What you don't want your kids to know I exist?"

Derrick kept a smile on his face while he spoke. "Listen bitch you acting real stupid right now you know that I'm married right? And you also know that my wife is my business partner right? So that means if my marriage gets messed up so does my business," he explained. "What is your problem?"

"My problem is you don't make me feel like a priority," Pearl said. "You make me feel like you coming to see me is hard work or something."

"So you figured you'd come and we we'd discuss this now," he said sarcastically.

"Well this is the only way I can get you to talk to me; you don't answer my calls anymore."

"Pearl go home and I'll see you when I get there."

"No you're going to talk to me now!" Pearl huffed. She knew if she left she might not have ever heard from Derrick again.

Derrick tried to keep his cool, but Pearl was making it extremely hard. He was trying his best to get rid of her without it turning into an argument or an altercation but from the looks of it, Pearl wasn't getting the message. "Baby can we please talk about this later?"

"Why can't we talk about it now?" Pearl pressed. "What you can't talk to me in public now?"

Derrick looked over at Tony and nodded his head. Tony quickly walked over and grabbed Pearl. "Come on Pearl, it's time for you to go."

"Get your fucking hands off me motherfucker!" Pearl yelled putting on a show as Tony and another man from Derrick's security escorted her out of the venue. It was an embarrassing scene.

Eric walked up. "Pop is everything alright?"

"Yeah I'm good," Derrick answered quickly.

Eric shook his head. "You know mom is going to kill you right?"

Derrick nodded. "Yeah I know." He could tell that Pearl wasn't going to take being kicked to the curb lightly. The last thing he needed was for Pearl to be acting like this. Derrick knew if Millie were home right now, this whole scene would have played out a lot different. A few minutes later one of Derrick's bodyguards walked up to him. "Sorry to bother you Mr. Mason but your services are needed out front."

Derrick stepped out front and saw Pearl acting a fool, she was cursing, swinging on his security causing a huge scene and drawing a bunch of unwanted attention. Derrick walked up, firmly grabbed, Pearl, and shook her. "Calm down!"

"No fuck you Derrick!" Pearl yelled as tears streamed down her face. "Any time you call me I'm always there for you and all I'm asking is that you treat me like you care, like I'm not just some chick you're sleeping with."

"How the fuck do you expect me to treat you like a lady when you're acting like an animal?"

"So that's all I am to you, an animal?" Pearl looked up at, Derrick. "Look me in my face and tell me you never loved me."

Derrick shook his head. All he wanted was for Pearl to leave and do it quietly, but instead she chose to cause a big scene all for nothing. "Get in the car with my security and let them take you home."

"Come with me," Pearl begged. "We need to talk come home with me so we can get to the bottom of this, you at least owe me that much."

"I don't owe you nothing," Derrick snapped. He was just about to dismiss Pearl when he notice a motorcycle zoom down the street. Hanging off the back of the bike was a man dressed in all black with a ski mask covering his face. "Get down!" Derrick yelled as he tackled, Pearl down to the concrete as the sound of rapid gunfire erupted. Derrick laid on the ground as he watched his men drop like flies. By the time that his men got ready to return fire, the bike was long gone. Derrick quickly hopped back to his feet. "Get out of here now!" He yelled as he shoved Pearl towards the awaiting vehicle.

"You good?" Tony asked as him and another bodyguard quickly escorted Derrick in the back of his awaiting vehicle. As soon as Derrick's butt hit the seat, the truck pulled off. "Did you get a good look at the shooter?"

"No need it was one of the Lopez brothers," Derrick said in a calm tone. He knew there was a contract on his head and was expecting the hit men to make their first move too bad for them because Derrick was still alive. "Let the games begin."

MIKE

28

"You like that don't you?" Mike said in a smooth sexy tone. Lying flat on her stomach butt naked was, Nicole Alvarez. Mike straddled her lower back, giving her a much-needed strong-handed massage.

"Yes baby I love it," Nicole moaned. "First you fuck my brains out then I get a massage what's the catch?"

"No catch, I just want to make sure my queen is well taken care of," Mike told her as he worked his way down to her feet, the soft jazz music that flowed softly through the speakers made for an even more relaxed atmosphere. In the last few months, Mike had really fallen in love with Nicole but he couldn't just sit around and let her try and destroy his entire family, he loved her a lot, but he loved his family more. His last name may have been Brown but at the end of the day, he was still a Mason. "So any word on the Lopez Twins?"

"Not yet last I heard they made it to town last night," Nicole said with her eyes closed. "I heard they like to work in silence so I'm just going to sick back and let them do their job."

"I want you to stay out of it baby," Mike said. "I don't know what I would do if something happened to you."

"Trust me I'm going to be fine from what I hear the Lopez Twins are professionals," Nicole said confidently. She made sure she kept her phone close hoping it would ring with some good news.

Mike continued to massage Nicole's back when he noticed the room door slowly ease open and three men entered the room. "I love you Nicole," Mike said as he got up and stood to his feet.

"Aww baby I love you way mo..." Nicole turned on her back and her words got caught in her throat when she looked up and saw Jimmy, Big foot, and Derrick standing over her bed, all three men held a silence gun in their hand. "Mike what's this all about?"

"Bitch you know damn well what this is all about," Mike said in a cold tone. "I want you to meet my family, Derrick and Jimmy Mason."

Nicole's mouth hung open in shock. "Mike how could you do this to me?"

"Nothing personal but business is business," Mike said. His tone was flat as if Nicole was a stranger from off the street and not the woman he was just making plans to be with.

"My father always told me there's two things in this world you never trust and that's a thief and a nigger," Nicole said letting the last word roll off her tongue.

Derrick's arm moved in a blur as his pistol-whipped Nicole. Jimmy and Mike looked on as they watched their father rearrange Nicole's once beautiful face. "Fuck you talking to like that!" He stood over her breathing heavily.

Nicole laid on the bed, her face badly bruised and covered in blood. "My uncle, Victor Alvarez will avenge me and my father's death," she said as she held up her middle finger.

"Fuck you and your uncle," Derrick raised his arm, squeezed the trigger, and watched Nicole's brain splatter all over the white wall. Jimmy followed up and fired four shots into Nicole's chest.

Derrick walked up to Mike and looked him in the eyes. "You did the right thing son and I'm proud of you."

"Thank you," Mike said as tears threatened to spill from his watery eyes. He couldn't believe that Nicole was actually dead. All she was trying to do was avenge her father's death. Derrick quickly pulled Mike in for a hug. Mike rested his head on Derrick's shoulder and cried his eyes out. He had just lost the first woman he ever truly loved all because Jimmy couldn't control his temper.

Mike exited the hotel and just sat in his car for a while he had a lot to think about. His life was beginning to spiral out of control and he didn't like it. He chose to help contribute to the family business to help the family make as much money as possible and keep his loved ones out of jail. Making money was one thing but murder was a whole different type of beast. Mike didn't sign up to become a murderer. A strong knock on the driver's window snapped Mike out of his thoughts. He quickly rolled the window down and looked up at Derrick.

"You sure you going to be alright?" Derrick asked. He knew Mike watching his girlfriend get murdered in cold blood was going to mess with his head for a while.

"Yeah I'm good," Mike said looking straight ahead right now he couldn't even look at Derrick.

"She was trying to take down our entire family you did what you had to do."

Mike nodded his head. Everything Derrick was saying went in one ear and out the other.

"Mike this wasn't personal you do know that right?"

Mike looked up at Derrick. "Yeah I know business is business," he said, then pulled recklessly out of the parking lot leaving Derrick standing there.

MR. GOLDBERG

29

"Yes I'm here to see a Mr. Chambers," Mr. Goldberg said to the receptionist in the expensive looking office building.

"Just one minute sir," the brunette hair woman picked up the phone, spoke a few words, hung up, then looked up and smiled. "Mr. Chambers will be with you in a second."

Mr. Goldberg sat in the waiting area and sat his briefcase down. Normally at this time of the day, he would have been in the courtroom, but not today. Today he had other business to attend to for the Mason Family.

"Mr. Chambers will see you now sir," the brunette announced. "Right this way." She led Mr. Goldberg down a long hallway until she reached the office they were looking for. The brunette raised her fist and knocked on the door, almost instantly the voice on the other side of the door replied. "Come in!"

Mr. Goldberg entered the office with a smile on his face. "Mr. Chambers?"

"Yes that would be me."

"Mr. Goldberg, I'm counsel for the Mason Family," he extended his hand.

"I know who you are I see you on the news all the time," Mr. Chambers shook Mr. Goldberg's hand. "So how can I help you?"

"I'm here on the behalf of my client, Eric Mason," Mr. Goldberg began. "My client is willing to make you an outstanding offer to buy one of your hotels."

"My hotels are not for sale," Mr. Chambers said.

"My client told me to tell you that he's willing to make you an offer you cannot refuse," Mr. Goldberg smiled.

"What are you deaf or something?" Mr. Chambers barked. "I just told you my hotels are not for sell."

"I really think you should reconsider," Mr. Goldberg smiled. "I don't think that's what you want me to go back and tell Mr. Mason."

"You listen to me you son of a bitch!" Mr. Chambers yelled as he stood to his feet. "I know all about the Mason Family and I want nothing to do with a family full of criminals!" Mr. Chambers wasn't a fan of the Mason Family and didn't want his name linked nowhere near that family and all of their problems. "Don't come in my office trying to muscle me because I'm telling you right now you don't want to fuck with me I'm well connected," he snapped. "There's no way I'm going to let any Mason buy my chain of hotels."

"Mr. Mason doesn't want to buy your chain of hotels all he wants is one."

"It starts off with one then the next thing you know in a few years that one would turn into five, then ten, then before you know it I'm out of business," Mr. Chambers huffed. "I've seen how this movie ends and I want nothing to do with the Mason Family."

Mr. Goldberg stood to his feet and popped opened his briefcase. Inside was a contract. "I strongly urge you to sign this," Mr. Goldberg held out the sheet of paper.

Mr. Chambers snatched the paper from his hand and ripped it up into little pieces. "Fuck you and this contract!"

Mr. Goldberg smiled. "Thank you for your time." He turned and made his exit leaving Mr. Chambers standing there with a lot to think about.

KELLY

30

Kelly walked throughout her hotel room in nothing but a bra and a pair of boy shorts. In her hand was a glass of wine it was only midday and she was already working on her second bottle. Kelly couldn't believe that Eric really wouldn't allow her back into their house. After all the years they had been together she figured, Eric would have forgiven her by now but she was wrong. Kelly noticed the change in Eric ever since he caught her fooling around with Jimmy. It was as if the situation had turned Eric cold, he was no longer the goody two shoe in the family. Kelly had flipped Eric's violent switch on. She knew Eric was a good guy and she knew it was her fault why they weren't together but that was something she would have to eat. Kelly picked up her cell phone and dialed Jimmy's number. The phone rung three times then went straight to voicemail. "Shit!" She cursed. For the past few weeks, Kelly wasn't able to get in touch with Jimmy and it pissed her off. At first, Kelly was worried that something bad may have happened to Jimmy but when she logged on to Instagram and saw him posting pictures with other women, her worry quickly turned into anger. "I ruined my life for him and he think he's just going to ignore my calls? I don't think so," she said out loud to no one particular, she threw on a pair of jeans, a t-shirt and, slipped her feet in a pair of Uggs. Kelly grabbed her keys off the nightstand and headed out the door. She hopped in her Range Rover and head straight to Jimmy's house. During the ride, Kelly had plenty of time to think about the situation and the more she thought about it the worse she felt. At the end of the day, Eric was a good guy and didn't deserve that. Kelly thought about trying to talk to Eric and maybe try and work out their problems but now it was too late because Eric was no longer taking her calls. Kelly snapped out of her thoughts when she pulled up to Jimmy's mansion and saw a car that she didn't recognize out front. Kelly stepped out the car, walked up to the front door and rang the bell. Seconds later, Jimmy answered the door shirtless.

"Yo what up?" Jimmy asked.

"Damn I don't get no hug or nothing?" Kelly huffed. As soon as Jimmy opened the door, the scent of a woman's perfume flooded the air. Kelly could tell that something wasn't right just from how suspicious Jimmy looked.

Jimmy leaned over and gave Kelly and one-handed church hug. "What you doing over here?"

"Um I came over here to see my man," Kelly said in a matter of fact tone. "It's kind of chilly out here, you going to invite me inside?" She asked with a raised brow.

"Nah I'm a little busy right now," Jimmy said in an uninterested tone. He was starting to catch feelings with Kelly until he realized if she treated Eric the way she did then it was no telling what she would do to him. "And don't just be popping up to my crib like that, you better call first next time."

"I did but you must have been too busy to answer your phone."

"What do you want, Kelly?"

"Why are you treating me like this?" Kelly asked as her began to water.

"You shitted on my brother, what you thought I was gon wife you up so you could do the same thing to me? Fuck outta here," Jimmy huffed his tone showed no respect.

"Who is she?" Kelly asked.

"Huh?"

"Who's the bitch what's her name?" Kelly growled.

"It's time for you to go," before Jimmy could say another word, a woman with a huge ass appeared behind him.

"Daddy you good?" Stoney asked. She was a big booty stripper that Jimmy had been dealing with on the side for a while. She loved Jimmy to death and would do anything for him. Stoney stepped outside with an aggravated looked on her face whoever this white girl was, she was interfering with her and Jimmy's sex time, and that was a problem.

"Nah I told shorty she gotta bounce but she ain't trying to hear that," Jimmy said. He knew his words were sure to start a problem.

"Listen it's time for you to go sweetie," Stoney said in a stern tone. From just looking at the white girl, she could tell that she was trouble.

"I'm sorry but I wasn't talking to you!" Kelly snapped.

Stoney shook her head as she pulled her hair back into a ponytail. Just as Kelly got ready to say another word, Stoney crept up and punched Kelly in the side of the head. "Bitch I said it was time for you to bounce!" Stoney growled as she violently slung Kelly down to the ground by her hair. She planted her knee down into Kelly's chest and repeatedly punched her in her exposed face.

Jimmy sat back and laughed as he watched Kelly get beat as if she stole something. He felt a little bad but brushed it off when he thought about how grimy she was. After watching, Kelly get beat on for five minutes Jimmy finally stepped in and decided to get Stoney off of Kelly. "Chill ma you gon fuck around and kill her."

"Bitch I said bounce!" Stoney spat as she watched Kelly wobble back to her Range Rover.

Jimmy smirked as he watched Kelly climb in her truck and pull off of his property.

MIKE

31

Mike walked down the street with his hands in his pocket and his head down. In the neighborhood he was in the last thing he wanted to be was seen. Walking close behind him were two men that worked for the family. Mike entered the building he was looking for and took the stairs to the fourth floor. Mike stepped out the staircase and pulled a .45 from his waistband, the two goons that flanked him followed his lead. When Mike reached the apartment that he was looking for he aimed his gun at the lock and pulled the trigger.

BOOM!

Immediately the two goons ran inside the apartment guns blazing. Mike entered the apartment last and saw drugs, money, and dead bodies everywhere. Out the corner of his eye, Mike spotted a figure coming from the kitchen; he spun and dropped the man with four shots to the chest. Mike eased his way down the hall until he heard the words, "Clear!" Get yelled out repeatedly.

Mike walked to the back room and found a closet full of perfectly packaged bricks of cocaine. "Jackpot!" Mike said with a smile. His informant's information had paid off lovely. The Mason Family had no more product coming in, so Mike had to go out and find a way to get some product. "Bag all of this up and let's get out of here," he said as the two goons did as they were told. Mike knew he had a lot to lose if he got caught but he couldn't just sit back and let the family sink. He knew if the Mason Family didn't have any drugs then it wouldn't be long before some other crews tried to take over their territory and that was something he refused to let happen. Over the years, he had watched Derrick and Millie work their asses off to gain, keep, and control their territory. Once the two goons were done, the trio quickly made their exit.

Mike dropped the two goons off in front of their project building, paid them both $10,000 apiece then pulled off and headed to his father's mansion. Mike knew that Derrick would be proud of him when he saw how much produce he was able to get his hands on. He pulled up in front of the mansion, killed the engine, and headed inside. Mike walked pass the security and found Derrick on an intense phone conversation. He helped himself to a seat and waited for his father to get off the phone.

Derrick got off the phone with a mean look on his face. "That damn Millie is going to drive me crazy I swear."

Mike chuckled. "What she complaining about now?"

"Worried about Eric," Derrick shook his head. "She heard about the shooting at the charity event now she's in jail worrying herself to death I swear she loves that boy way more than she loves me."

"You know how Millie is pop," Mike said. "But I have some news that'll be sure to put a smile on your face."

"I'm listening."

"I just got us enough product to last us for about a month," Mike said proudly.

Derrick pulled Mike close and hugged him tight. "That's what I'm talking about we have to keep our territory by any means necessary," he said in a strong whisper. "Everyone is watching us to see how we handle this so we have to stand strong."

"I got you pop. I'll work on the next month's product in a week or two."

Derrick draped his arm around Mike's neck. "I appreciate everything you've been doing. This family wouldn't have made it this far without you," he paused. "And I know you still a little sad about what happened to your girlfriend I just want you to know that it wasn't personal it was business."

"I understand pop," Mike smiled. "I have a few things I need to take care of. I just wanted to drop and tell you the good news."

"Thank you son. I appreciate you," Derrick said as he watched his adopted son make his exit.

ERIC

32

E ric sat on his leather sofa with his feet kicked up on the coffee table thinking about how much his life had changed in just a few weeks. Catching his wife cheating on him changed his entire thought process and had him looking at life differently. All his life, Eric had been doing everything by the book and it hadn't gotten him nowhere. Now with him taking on a more violent approach, he immediately noticed the change from how people treated him to how they spoke to him it was as if his respect level had elevated and Eric was enjoying being treated like a man for once and not some flunky. Eric looked down and heard his cell phone vibrating on the coffee table he looked down at the screen and saw Mr. Goldberg's name flashing across the screen. "Tell me something good," he answered.

"He wouldn't budge," Mr. Goldberg said. "I think he needs to see firsthand what the Mason Family is all about."

SILK WHITE

"I'll take care of it," Eric told him and ended the call. Eric stood to his feet and quickly got dressed. A face-to-face meeting with Mr. Chambers was needed. Eric returned back downstairs dressed in an expensive looking black Ferragamo suit. He grabbed his cell phone off the coffee table when he heard a loud knock at his front door. Eric walked over to the front door and snatched it open expecting to see Kelly standing on the other side. She had been calling him nonstop every day for the past couple of weeks. Eric was ready to curse Kelly out but stopped when he saw a six' five" beast with a teardrop tattoo on his face standing on the other side of the door. "Can I help you?"

"You, Eric?" The big man asked.

"Yeah why?"

The big hand extended his hand, handing Eric a cell phone. Eric took the phone and put it up to his ear. "Hello?"

"Hey son it's me."

"Mommy?"

"You don't know your mother's voice by now?" Millie joked. "That man standing at your door step is a good friend of mine his name is Pistol Pete. I heard about the problems that your brother and father has

148

gotten the entire family into so Pistol Pete is going to protect you."

"Thanks ma but I can handle myself," Eric said quickly. "I'm not a baby anymore."

"You're always going to be my baby," Millie corrected him. "And what's all this news I'm hearing about you out there carrying a gun?"

"Can't believe everything you hear ma."

"Eric this life isn't for you, I didn't raise you like this," Millie said. "You're better than this, much better than this."

"I know ma it's just I'm tired people not respecting me or taking me serious." Eric told her.

"Listen to me Eric this isn't the way to get respect all I'm asking is that you stay out of trouble until mamma comes home and I'll take care of everything," Millie said. "You are the most valuable person in this family because your hands are clean, no matter what promise me that you'll keep your hands clean."

"I promise."

Millie knew that this was a dirty game and the last thing she wanted to see was her son get caught up in some foolishness. "And I want you to go and apologize to your brother."

"Apologize to him? He should be apologizing to me."

"You harmed your blood over someone that wasn't blood you owe him an apology," Millie explained. "I don't ever wanna hear about you going against the family for an outsider ever again that's not what we do because at the end of the family is all we got."

"You right ma," Eric said. After listening to Millie, she made some good points and gave him a lot to think about. "I have to go take care of something."

"Okay son you be careful out there," Millie said then ended the call. Eric turned and handed Pistol Pete back his phone. "So what's your story?"

"Just here to watch over you," Pistol Pete said simply. He was an intimidating looking man. Just from looking at him, Eric could tell that he enjoyed violence and had been to jail more than once. "I promised your mother that I would look after you until she's released."

"So what are you supposed to like follow me around everywhere I go?"

Pistol Pete nodded.

"Good I have a meeting downtown and we have to get going," Eric said as they climbed inside Pistol Pete's bulletproof Cadillac truck.

* * *

Mr. Chambers sat behind his desk looking at some documents when his office door busted open and Eric and Pistol Pete walked in.

"Can I help you gentlemen?" Mr. Chambers said with a nervous look on his face.

"Eric Mason," Eric extended his hand. Mr. Chambers hesitated for a second before shaking Eric's hand.

"My lawyer tells that you had a problem with my proposition," Eric helped himself to a seat.

"Yes my chain of hotels are not for sell."

"I just want to buy one, not all of them," Eric countered.

"I've worked my ass off to get these hotels and you or no lawyer are going to talk me out of it," Mr. Chambers stood his ground.

"I'm willing to make you an offer you can't refuse," Eric said. He hated people like Mr. Chambers the type of man that had way more than enough and refused to give other people a crumb. Eric pulled out a sheet of paper from the folder he held. "Here's the contract and you're going to sign it."

"Fuck you!" Mr. Chambers spat. He refused to let a family full of criminals have a piece of his empire. Before Mr. Chambers knew what was going on, Pistol Pete had slapped him across the face, grabbed him by the back of his neck and shoved his face down into the desk, then pressed a gun to the back of his head.

Eric smiled. "You have two choices, choice number one you can sign this contract with a pen or choice number two I'll sign it for you in your blood you choose."

Mr. Chambers picked up a pen from off his desk and signed the contract. He looked up from the paper with a scowl on his face. "I'm never going to let you get away with this," he said with venom dripping from his tone. If looks could kill, Eric would have died a horrible death. "I'll come after you and make you pay if it's the last thing that I do."

Eric nodded. "I'll look forward to seeing you again."

Mr. Chambers stared a hole in Eric's back as him and his bodyguard made their exit.

JIMMY

33

"This ain't going to last me for the whole week I'm going to need more," the worker said.

"Patience," Jimmy told him. "Before you run out I'll have more product for you." Product was running low and streets were in need of a big shipment if the Mason Family didn't find a new connect fast they risked the possibility of other dealers trying to take over their turf. Jimmy stood in the stash house and looked around at how empty it was. At one point and time they had to use the entire apartment building as a stash house, now all they needed was one apartment. Jimmy and Big foot got ready to leave when the worker stopped him.

"I know it's none of my business but the streets is talking," the worker said.

"What are they saying?"

"Word on the streets is the Mason Family is finished in this business," the worker began. "I've been hearing other crews talk about moving in on y'all's territory."

"They ain't stupid," Big foot snapped. He didn't like what he was hearing.

"The streets is saying that the Mason Family is weak now that the big bosses cut y'all off," the worker said. "They saying its open season on any Mason so make sure y'all stay on point."

"Thanks for the info," Jimmy said as he watched the worker make his exit. Hearing about how people felt about his family pissed Jimmy off.

"Don't pay that shit no mind the streets can talk all they want if anybody steps foot on our territory we going to show them just how powerful we are," Big foot said as him and Jimmy exited the stash house.

Jimmy stepped on the elevator with a frown on his face. If the streets were saying the Mason Family was soft then he was going to have to let them know otherwise. Jimmy and Big foot stepped out the building when a motorcycle zoomed past with Danny Lopez hanging off the back of the bike. Once Jimmy and Big Foot were in the line of fire he squeezed down on the trigger turning the once quiet street into what sounded like a war zone.

"Get down!" Big foot yelled as he tried to rush to push Jimmy out of harm's way, but machine gun bullets ripped through his shoulder, wind milling him violently down to the ground. Jimmy dove behind a parked car as bullets tore into the vehicle showering his head with broken glass. Jimmy pulled his gun from his holster but by the time, he made it to his feet, Danny Lopez, and the motorcycle was long gone. "Shit!"

Jimmy walked over and looked down at Big foot it hurt his heart to see his friend laying on the ground in pain. "You alright?"

"Yeah I'm good," Big foot said as he removed his pistol from his waist and handed it to Jimmy. "The cops will be here any second get out of here you don't need no more trouble."

Jimmy nodded, took the gun, walked over, and hopped in his car, then pulled off leaving his friend on the ground bleeding. As Jimmy drove away from the scene, he saw several cop cars zoom past him flying in the opposite direction. Big foot was a soldier so Jimmy knew he would be good.

When Jimmy got home, he saw Stoney standing over the stove wearing a wife beater and a red thong frying some chicken. "Damn," Jimmy moaned as he walked up and slapped Stoney's ass just so he could watch it jiggle.

"Hey baby," Stoney turned and kissed Jimmy on the lips. "Making you some fried chicken."

"Good cause I'm starving. How was your day?"

"It was okay," Stoney was working at the strip club to save up $250,000 so she could buy her dream home and invest the rest in a profitable business. So far, she had $110,000 saved away. "You better talk to that white bitch because she going to make me hurt her."

"Why what happened?"

"That bitch been calling the motherfucking house all day," Stoney said with an attitude. "You better talk to her before I hurt her."

Jimmy shrugged. "I ain't talking to nobody so do what you gotta do."

ERIC

34

Eric walked inside the five-star restaurant with Pistol Pete close on his heels. Right now, Eric needed a good meal and a few drinks in his system he had been running around so much that he had forgotten to eat. As Eric was being escorted to his table he spotted two beautiful women sitting alone at a table. "Excuse me ladies would you to like to join me and my friend for some drinks?"

"Sure the dark skin one out of the two said," she and her friend got up and followed Eric and Pistol Pete to a low-key booth that sat in the back.

"I'm Eric," Eric said extending his hand.

"Wendy," The dark skin chick replied as she shook Eric's hand. "And that there is my friend Monica."

"Nice to meet you both," Eric said as he ordered a few bottles of wine. "So tell me a little about yourself."

"Well I'm twenty nine years old, I work at a nursing home, and I like to have fun," Wendy smiled. She favored the singer K. Michelle in the looks department. "How about yourself?"

Eric watched the waiter sit the bottles of wine down on the table before he spoke. "Well I work for myself and have several companies that I own, I also like to have fun and enjoy myself."

"How old are you?"

"Twenty eight," Eric answered.

"You seemed to have accomplished a lot in a short period of time," Wendy smiled. "You single?"

"Married but I will be divorced real soon."

"Sorry to hear that."

"It's okay," Eric sipped his wine. While Wendy spoke, he was checking her out and he liked what he saw. Over on the other side of the table, Pistol Pete was holding his own with Wendy's friend.

Eric and Wendy sipped wine and got to know one another when out of nowhere a drunken man with a big bushy beard approached their table.

"Excuse me is this your wife?" The man with the beard asked.

The question caught, Eric off guard. "Excuse me?"

"I was just wondering what she is to you," the man with the beard said. "Is she your wife?"

"Nah she's my friend."

"What kind of friend?" The man with the beard pressed.

"Fuck does it matter to you?" Eric said getting upset. He couldn't believe the man had the audacity to come over to his table and ask him about a chick that he was with.

"I was just asking because I had my eye on her," The bearded man said with no shame. He turned his gaze on Wendy. "What's good ma, come holla at a real nigga?"

With the quickness of a cat, Eric jumped to his feet, grabbed the wine bottle from off the table, and busted it over the bearded man's head sending shattered glass flying everywhere. Before Eric got a chance to follow up Pistol Pete stepped in and finished the bearded man off as he grabbed one of the tables in the restaurant, lifted it over his head, then violently tossed it down on the bearded man's head. When the scuffle broke out several patrons got up and quickly filed for the exit.

Eric pulled a card out of his pocket and handed to Wendy. "Sorry I have to go call me," he said as him and Pistol Pete disappeared out the front door of the restaurant.

DANNY LOPEZ

35

"Hit me!" Danny Lopez shouted to the bartender. He had been at the bar drinking for the past two hours, the bar was getting ready to close but he could care less. After finding out that his brother was dead, Danny ran to the nearest bar to drink his sorrows away. Killing Derrick Mason was no longer business it had now became personal.

"Closing in twenty," The bartender announced.

Danny nodded and downed the rest of his drink. He looked around and noticed that it was only him, another customer and, the bartender left in the bar.

The bartender glanced towards the entrance when he saw Mike enter the bar along with two other rough looking men. He called Mike when he recognized the man at the bar as the hit man that was hired to eliminate, Derrick Mason. He knew the reward would be worth the mess they would make in his place of business.

Mike walked right up to Danny Lopez and shot him in the back of his head spilling the man's brains all over the bar top. Seconds later another gunshot rang out. Mike looked to his left and saw that one of his henchmen had put a bullet in the back of the remaining customer's head. "Sorry about the mess," Mike said as he tossed the bartender a small pouch that contained $10,000 in cash inside.

"Any time," the bartender said with a grateful look on his face. It wasn't often that he was able to make $10,000 in one day.

"You guys clean this mess up," Mike ordered as he took a seat on one of the stools, reached over the counter, and poured himself a drink. He had finally gotten rid of both Lopez Twins now; Derrick didn't have to keep looking over his shoulder. Lately, Mike had been working around the clock to find some product for the family for the last few days the, Mason family had been completely out of product and the pressure was on for them to find something quickly before some crew got brave and tried to ease their way into their territory. Mike turned on his stool as he watched his crew roll, Danny Lopez's dead body up in a sheet of plastic and carry him out the back door. Mike had one last drink, turned and shook the bartender's hand, then left.

JIMMY

36

Jimmy laid on the bed as he watched Stoney's head bob up and down between his legs. He closed his eyes and enjoyed the loud wet, slurping sounds that, Stoney's mouth made. Jimmy held Stoney's hair with one hand making sure to keep it out of her face. "Damn!" He groaned as Stoney began bobbing her head faster and faster, as she released loud drawn out moans like she had the devil in her. Stoney refused to release Jimmy's tool until he filled her mouth his juices.

"Argh!" Jimmy groaned. That was just what he needed. He loved the way Stoney handled her business in the bedroom her skills made, Kelly seem like an amateur. Jimmy switched positions and got ready to return the favor when he heard someone ringing his doorbell.

"Don't answer it baby," Stoney wined she knew Jimmy had to go handle some business in the next few minutes and didn't want to miss out on her orgasm.

Jimmy ignored her as he grabbed his gun off the dresser and headed downstairs to see who had showed up to his house unannounced. Jimmy looked through the peephole and his whole mood changed instantly. He snatched the door open and saw Eric standing on the other side.

"I should blow your head off right now," Jimmy growled as he raised his gun aiming it at his brother's head.

"I'm here to apologize," Eric said with his hands raised in surrender. Before he could get another word out, Pistol Pete sprang from around the corner with his gun trained on Jimmy.

"Pete chill hold your fire!" Eric ordered.

"Who the fuck is that?" Jimmy asked turning his gun on the gunman.

"That's my new body guard that ma hired to keep me safe," Eric explained he then turned and faced Pistol Pete. "Pete put your gun down," he ordered.

"You two clowns got five seconds to get off my property," Jimmy warned. Thoughts of blowing Eric's head off crossed his mind, but the only reason he didn't shoot him was the simple fact that he felt bad for ruining his brother's marriage.

"I'm here to apologize," Eric said. "I was wrong for shooting you I reacted off of emotion and wasn't thinking clearly."

Jimmy lowered his gun. "You owe me a new shirt," he smiled and pulled Eric in for a hug. "It's good to see you."

"Likewise," Eric smiled. "Jimmy this is Pistol Pete, Pistol Pete Jimmy," he introduced the two.

"Pops told me you've been handling a few things for the family business," Jimmy smiled. He was having a hard time believing the stories about his baby brother living and acting like the rest of the family. "You know, Millie is going to kill you and pop when she finds out that you're getting your hands dirty out here in these streets."

"I know but the family needs me right now and I'm tired of just sitting around going over numbers all day," Eric explained. "Plus right now pop needs all the help he can get." Eric knew he wasn't supposed to be getting involved with this aspect of the business but it was something about the lifestyle that attracted and kept pulling him in.

"Speaking of help I think I may need you and Pistol Pete's help," Jimmy said.

"What you need?" Eric asked with a curious look on his face.

"I just got a call from Mike. He got the drop on a new shipment of cocaine that's coming in today," Jimmy said. "I have a few guys rolling out with me but if I had you two watching my back I'd feel a lot more comfortable."

"Where's Big foot?"

"Took one in the shoulder the other day," Jimmy told him.

"Tell me more about this shipment," Eric said in a serious tone.

"There's this truck coming in and it's supposed to be loaded with work," Jimmy explained.

"So what's the plan?"

"We going to hijack the whole truck," Jimmy said his tone was all business.

"I don't know this sounds risky," Eric rubbed the top of his head. He was still a beginner and was scared that maybe he was biting off more than he could chew with this job.

"This job is going to be a piece of cake," Jimmy smiled. "Mike is going to pull the truck over kill the driver, and then we pull up and take the truck in and out."

"How many men in the truck?" Pistol Pete asked.

"Just the driver."

"You sure?" Pistol Pete asked. If he was going on the job, he needed to know everything about it.

"Positive," Jimmy turned and faced Eric. "We have to take this truck we've been dead for the last week."

"Completely dead like no drugs what so ever?"

"Completely dead," Jimmy repeated with a look of stress on his face. "Either we get this shipment or we lose all of our territory and everything that our family has built for years," Jimmy looked over at Eric and Pistol Pete. "Are y'all in or what?"

MIKE

37

For the past thirty minutes, Mike had been following the delivery truck. The family was depending on the contents in the back of that truck; Mike cruised at a decent speed. He had to wait until the truck made it to a certain checkpoint spot before pulling it over. Mike's palms were sweaty and his stomach was doing flips. If the stuff that Mike had been doing ever got out he knew he would be finished. A part of Mike actually wouldn't mind if the family had went legit, it wasn't as they weren't already filthy rich. "Here we go!" Mike said out loud trying to pump himself up, he reached down and hit his lights signaling for the driver of the truck to pull over. Mike watched as the truck driver hit his signal light as the truck began to slow down and shift over to the side of the rode. Once the truck was at a complete stop, Mike pulled out his cell phone, sent a text message, then stepped out of his vehicle and approached the truck.

The truck driver rolled his window down and stuck his head out. "What seems to be the problem officer?"

Mike removed a silence .380 from the small of his back, climbed up the steps that led to the driver's door, stuck his arm in the window, and blew the driver's head off. Mike hopped down and quickly walked back to his vehicle, hopped in, and drove off as if nothing happened.

One minute later a black Cadillac truck pulled up and three men dressed in all black with ski mask covering their faces hopped out while the driver stayed behind the wheel.

"I'm going to clean the blood off the windshield you two go check the back," Jimmy ordered as he headed for the front of the truck.

Pistol Pete and one of Jimmy's goons a man that went by the name, Joe headed to the back to make sure the drugs were there. Joe opened the back door to the truck and immediately his eyes opened wide in shock when he saw a Mexican man standing there with a machine gun in his hands. Before Joe could even say a word his body riddled with bullets.

Eric sat behind the wheel of the Cadillac truck and watched the Mexican man murder Joe in cold blood. "Shit!"

Pistol Pete stood on the side of the truck, stuck his Mack 10 inside, and squeezed down on the trigger. He waved his arm back and forth until he heard the sound of a body dropping to the floor. Pistol Pete turned the corner, hopped on the back of the truck, and put eight more bullets into the Mexican man's body.

"What happened?" Jimmy asked as he ran around to the back of the truck.

"Nothing we good," Pistol Pete said as he violently tossed the Mexican's dead body off the truck.

Jimmy spun around and saw a cop car pull up to a screeching stop. Without thinking twice, Jimmy raised his Uzi and dumped an entire clip into the squad car's front windshield. "I think he called it in we have to move!"

Eric pulled the Cadillac truck up backwards so the back of the Cadillac truck was butt to butt with the truck. "We have to dump as much product in here as we can. We only have about three minutes," he announced. If the dead officer had called it in, that meant that every cop in the city would soon be looking for the delivery truck. Jimmy quickly hopped on the back of the truck as he and Pistol Pete quickly unloaded as much product as they could into the back of the Cadillac truck.

"Come on, come on, come on," Eric whispered with a scared look on his face. This was his first time in a serious life or death situation.

"Fuck!" Jimmy huffed when he saw that the Cadillac truck was full and there were still plenty more drugs on the truck. "Fuck that we taking our chances with the truck."

"Don't be greedy let's go!" Eric yelled.

"Get out of here we're taking the truck!" Jimmy said as he hopped down from the back of the truck and ran towards front and hopped in the driver's seat. There was way too much money on that truck for him just to leave it.

Eric pulled back onto the highway and gunned the engine; he wanted nothing to do with that truck.

Pistol Pete pulled the back doors closed on the truck as he felt the truck take off. He quickly reloaded his Mack 10 and took a seat on one of the crates.

As Jimmy drove on the highway, his eyes kept looking over at the side mirrors making sure no cops were behind him. He knew this was a risky move, but the pressure was on and his family needed him to come through in the clutch and he refused to let them down. He drove ten minutes away to a warehouse that his family owned. Jimmy parked the truck in the warehouse, hopped out and yelled to the top of his lungs. "That's what the fuck I'm talking about!"

Pistol Pete hopped off the back of the truck with a smile on his while Eric and Mike sat over in the cut smiling. The family was now officially back in business.

DERRICK

38

Derrick paced back and forth in, Pearl's house as he listened to her apologize over and over again. He had love for Pearl but he had to let her go because he knew she wouldn't be able to handle playing the background.

"Can you stop walking back and forth and say something please," Pearl said. For the past thirty minutes, she had been apologizing and Derrick hadn't said a word.

"How much?"

"Huh?"

"I said how much?" Derrick repeated.

"How much for what?" Pearl asked with a confused look on her face.

"How much to make you go away forever?" Derrick said coldly. He would rather pay Pearl to leave the city than find her with a bullet in her head when Millie got released from prison.

"Excuse me?" Pearl snaked her neck. "How dare you offer me money to get rid of me?"

"Listen Pearl," Derrick began. "I love you, you know I do but, Millie will be home in a few months and I don't want to see nothing bad happen to you."

"I'm not afraid of Millie," Pearl said trying to sound strong.

"I know you're not baby but," Derrick paused for a second. "Millie will kill you and not think twice about it."

Pearl sat down on the couch and looked down at the floor. "You love her more than me don't you?"

"She's my wife."

"I'll leave town, and I'm not taking any money from you either," Pearl said as tears ran down her face. She loved Derrick with all her heart and wished they could have been together but the truth was she knew Derrick's heart was with Millie.

"Can I get a hug?" Derrick asked with his arms open.

"Just go Derrick," Pearl wiped her eyes. "Just leave and you never have to see me ag..." Before she could finish her sentence, a spray of bullets ripped through her chest tossing her down to the floor.

"Oh shit!" Derrick yelled as he dove down to the floor as bullets rained through the front door and windows. He listened closely as he heard his bodyguards returning fire on the gunmen. Derrick crawled over to Pearl's body. He was going to check for a pulse but when he saw all the bullets holes in her body, he knew that she was already gone. Derrick heard a loud boom as his body guard Tony came spilling through the front door.

"How many of them are out there?" Derrick asked.

"Too many!" Was Tony's response. "Come on we have to get out of here!" Tony led Derrick out the back door out into the back yard. With the agility of a teenage athlete, Derrick hopped the fence in point one seconds and took off in a sprint through the neighbor's yard. Derrick spotted two shadows coming around the corner, pulled out his .38, and put the two figures down immediately. Derrick ran through another back yard when out of nowhere a gunman dove off the roof of the single-family home on to, Derrick's back. The two men hit the ground hard. Before Derrick could make it back to his feet, the gunman landed two hard blows to his face. The gunman went to throw another punch when Derrick scooped him up in the air and violently dumped him down on his head. In the mist of the scuffle, Derrick was able to grab his .38 from off the ground and get off two shots. Immediately the gunman stopped moving. Derrick looked back and saw Tony shooting it out with three different gunmen. It was either fight or flight and Derrick chose to take flight. He sprinted around the corner out into the street when out of nowhere a car hit him. Derrick's head bounced off the windshield as his momentum tossed him in the air. Derrick's body hung in the air for a few seconds before it came violently crashing down to the unforgiving concrete. The last thing Derrick remembered was seeing Tony get gunned down before everything went black.

JIMMY

39

Jimmy entered the building he was looking for, entered the staircase, and trotted up to the fourth floor. Jimmy stepped out of the staircase and slipped his hands into a pair of black gloves. He was finally getting around to taking out the witness who claimed to see his father murder two men in cold blood. Jimmy removed his silenced 9mm and shot the lock off the door. He barged through the front door with a two handed grip on his weapon. He eased his way through apartment when he came across an old lady who looked like someone's grandmother. Jimmy quickly put the old lady down with two shots to the chest.

Pst! Pst!

Jimmy moved throughout the apartment until he spotted his target standing in the kitchen frying some fish. He waited until she turned around before putting a bullet right between her eyes. Jimmy was already heading towards the exit before the woman's body hit the floor.

Jimmy made it back to his Benz when he heard his cell phone ringing he looked down and saw, Mike's name flashing across the screen. "What's up?" He answered.

"Meet me at the hospital now a team of hit men tried to kill pop," Mike said then hung up in Jimmy's ear.

* * *

Jimmy made it to the hospital and was ready to kill anyone who's last name wasn't Mason. He couldn't believe that someone was bold enough to try and kill, Derrick Mason. "What happen?"

"We don't have all the details yet," Eric said. "So far all I know is that pop has been hit by a car and took a bullet to the leg."

"Where's Mike?"

"If he showed up he would have blown his cover," Eric nodded towards all the police that were in the hospital waiting to have a word with Derrick Mason.

"You right, you right," Jimmy agreed. It was too risky for Mike to show his face in the hospital.

Twenty minutes later, the doctor came out and told Eric and Jimmy that they were allowed to go to the back and see their father.

"I'll be back in a second," Eric told Pistol Pete as he and Jimmy entered Derrick's room.

"Who did this to you?" Jimmy asked as soon as he stepped foot in the room. It really hurt him to see his father laid up in the hospital like this. "You think it was Danny Lopez?"

"No, Mike already took care of Danny for us," Derrick said in a light whisper. "I have no idea who could have been behind this."

"Think it could have been, Chico?" Eric asked. For some reason he didn't like or trust Chico.

"No if Chico was behind this I would be dead right now," Derrick told them. "I don't know who's behind this so until we figure this out I want everyone to stay on point."

"We got enough product to last us for a good while now," Jimmy said. He knew that would put a smile on his father's face.

Derrick smiled. "I knew I could depend on my boys to get things back on track." He got ready to say something else when they all heard a light knock at the door. Derrick looked over at the door and couldn't believe his eyes.

Jack Mason walked in the hospital room with a concerned look on his face. "I got here as soon as I heard what happened." Jack Mason was Derrick's older brother and the one who had started Derrick in the business it just so happen that Derrick learned the business met Millie who was already in the business and took it to a whole other level. Jack Mason was always jealous of Derrick's success. Word on the streets was it was Jack who had told on Millie and got her a fifteen-year sentence but Derrick refused to entertain that rumor. Derrick knew he couldn't trust Jack, so instead of killing his brother he just chose to stay away from him.

"When you get out?" Derrick asked.

"Been home for like two weeks now," Jack smiled. "It feels good to be back around family."

"Excuse me," Eric said as he exited the room. He had no words for Jack. For years, Millie had told him that Jack was no good and couldn't be trusted. Every time Jack came around, Eric made sure he excused himself just the thought of Jack being the one who put Millie behind bars made Eric want to put a bullet in his head.

"I heard about what's been going on out in these streets," Jack said. "Looks like I came home just in time."

"Thanks Jack but I have everything under control," Derrick said. The last thing he needed was Jack trying to stick his nose in his business.

"From where I'm standing it don't look like you have everything under control," Jack said. "Somebody out there wants you and your family dead. I don't think it'll be a bad idea for me and a few of my men to help look after the family at least until you fully recover."

"I have everything under control, Jack I thank you for extending a helping hand when I need it I'll call you," Derrick said. "Now if you don't mind I need to talk to my son about something real quick."

Jack nodded. "I just want you to know that if you need me I'm just a phone call away," he turned and exited the hospital room.

"I don't trust that motherfucker!" Jimmy spat once, Jack was out of earshot. "You should have let me kill him."

"He's irrelevant," Derrick said quickly. He didn't want his son losing focus on what was important and what wasn't. "I'm going to need you to hit the streets hard and let them know we back up and running."

"I got you," Jimmy nodded. "Also I took care of that witness situation too."

Derrick smiled. "I appreciate you stepping up to the plate while I'm in here."

"You already know," Jimmy said as he kissed his father on the cheek then left.

JACK MASON

40

Jack Mason exited the hospital, walked through the parking lot where one of his homeboys named Black leaned on the side of the car waiting for him. Without warning, Jack turned and smacked the shit out of Black. "I gave you a simple job; kill Derrick Mason."

"My men did their best," Black said rubbing the side of his face.

"How hard is it for ten armed men to kill one man?" Jack barked. With Derrick out of the picture, it would be that much easier for him to take over. "If you fuck up my opportunity to take over I promise I'll kill you myself," Jack said as him and Black slid in the car and pulled out of the hospital parking lot like a manic.

* * *

Black pulled up on the Alvarez estate and killed the engine. He and Jack walked up to the front door and rung the bell. Seconds later the butler answered the door and escorted the two men down the hall towards the den where Victor Alvarez sat smoking a cigar. He was the brother of Joey Alvarez.

"Jack it's nice to see you again," Victor Alvarez smiled. "I hope you have some good news for me," he took a long drag from his cigar.

"Unfortunately not," Jack said with a look of defeat on his face if it was one thing he hated it was looking stupid. "My men failed me but I can assure it that it won't happen again."

"How can I be so sure of that?" Victor asked with a raised brow. "I told you if you get rid of Derrick Mason, I'll introduce you to the big boss, Chico myself, and then you can control all of your brother's territory."

"I know and I promise you it will get done," Jack said. This was the opportunity he had been waiting for all his life. He hated that he had to kill his own brother to get on top but it was a dog eat dog business. Beside Jack had come to Derrick time and time again asking to be a part of the family business but each time he was denied the reason being he wasn't trust worthy and his decision-making skills were mediocre so for those two reason he was not allowed to partake in the family business. His family had shifted on him, now it was his turn to return the favor.

"You're going about this all the wrong way," Victor told him. "The strength and muscle of the family is Jimmy. Take him out, and the rest of the family will be a piece of cake."

Jack sat back and let Victor's words sink for a minute. He hated to admit but what Victor said was right. With Derrick in the hospital, Jimmy was now the heart and soul of the family. With, Jimmy eliminated from the picture would surely make Jack's job ten times easier. "Jimmy Mason will be dead before the week is out."

"Can I count on you?" Victor asked.

"I promise I won't let you down," Jack said as him and black stood and made their exit.

JIMMY

41

Jimmy parked his Benz in the strip club's parking lot and killed the engine. He stepped out of the car and stumbled before catching his balance for the past few hours he had been drinking nonstop. With so much going on, he needed something to calm his nerves.

"Yo, you good?" Big foot stepped out of the passenger side of the Benz. His arm was still in a sling and doctors told him that he needed to take it easy for a while but there was no way he could let Jimmy leave the house in this condition alone. His motto was sometimes you have to save people from themselves.

"I'm great," Jimmy lied. He told, Big foot that he was coming to pick, Stoney up from work but the truth of the matter was he was jealous and coming to her job just to be nosey looking for trouble. Jimmy made it to the front of the strip and him and Big foot were immediately searched and frisked before being allowed inside the strip club. Jimmy entered the strip club and scanned the scene from left to right. At first glance, he hadn't spotted Stoney. A crowd of men roaring with excitement and tossing bills into the air caught Jimmy's attention. He looked over and spotted Stoney on all fours shaking her ass in a few of the men's faces that stood around the counter. The closer Jimmy made it towards the counter the more he could see, Stoney's ass jiggling like Jello. The more the men applauded and tossed money the angrier Jimmy became. He sat back and watched as Stoney degraded herself as men tossed money down on her head as if she was worthless a few men even took it a step further and tossed their dollars in, Stoney's face in a disrespectful manner. Jimmy sat back and watched as Stoney ignored the blatant disrespect like the men watching her shake her ass didn't exist.

"Damn this bitch got the crazy fat ass!" One drunk man yelled and tossed a fist full of dollars at Stoney. He grabbed Stoney's oily butt cheeks but took it a step further and tried to slip one of his fingers in her ass. Stoney immediately moved and slapped the man's hand away and cursed him out. The drunk man paid her no mind and continued to eye her hungrily.

Stoney was about to slap the drunk man for trying to violate her but paused when she saw Jimmy making his way towards her.

Jimmy walked up to Stoney, grabbed her wrist, and escorted her down from the counter top. "Come here we need to talk!" He snapped.

"Damn where you going with my bitch!" The drunk man slurred loud enough to cause Jimmy to stop dead in his tracks and turn around.

"Fuck you just said?" Jimmy walked up on the drunk man and slapped the tasted out of his mouth. "You disrespecting my girl?" He raised his foot and stomped the man's head into the floor. "You tried to put a finger in her ass?" He stomped down on the man's head again. "You wanna fuck my bitch?" He stomped the man again. "Do you know who I am?" He stomped the drunk man's head down into the floor again. Jimmy raised his leg to stomp the man again when two bouncer roughly tackled him down to the floor. Without thinking twice, Stoney began swinging wildly on the bouncers. In the mist of the scuffle, Big foot grabbed a bottle and busted it over one of the bouncers head. The trio was roughly escorted outside and tossed out onto the curb like trash.

Jimmy stood to his feet and brushed himself off, then helped Stoney up to her feet. She got ready to curse the bouncers out but Jimmy quickly stopped her. "They'll be dead by the morning time."

Big foot peeled himself up off the ground and was about to join Jimmy and Stoney when he saw a car coasting at a low speed with the headlights off. He tried to warn Jimmy but it was too late. Two gunmen hung out the window and opened fire.

Bullets tore through Stoney as if her body was a wet napkin. The force from the shots flung her body back into Jimmy. He hit the ground as he heard the gunshots end and the loud sound of tires squealing. Jimmy rolled over and saw Stoney laid out with several bullet holes in her body. He looked over to his left and saw Big foot laid dead in the streets, his body decorated with multiple bullet wounds.

"Argggghhhhhh!" Jimmy yelled to the top of his lungs.

ERIC

42

Eric stood in the lobby of new hotel that he acquired from Mr. Chambers. It was a five-star establishment not far from the airport that had potential to make Eric a fortune. Eric walked through the hotel introducing himself to the entire staff he even met one on one with all of the maids. Eric turned and looked at Pistol Pete. "I want you to hire a security team and make sure that everyone feels safe when they walk in here," he then turned and faced the manager. "I want every one of our guest to be treated like they're the president, understood?"

Ryan nodded his head. He had been the manager at this very hotel for the past five years. "No problem."

"Also rooms 900 to 905 are off limits to guest as well as staff," Eric told him.

Ryan nodded. "You got it boss."

"Great," Eric smiled. "Any problems or anything make sure you call me first even before you call the cops. I'm putting you in charge of running this place don't let me down."

"I promise I won't let you down sir," Ryan said in a serious tone then went to go do his job.

"Think you can trust him?" Pistol Pete asked once Ryan was out of earshot.

"Not really but we'll use him until I can find somebody else a bit more solid." The last thing Eric needed was Ryan running around the hotel looking into things that didn't concern him. Eric looked out through front door of the hotel and saw one of his men pull his Cadillac truck up to the front door. "Make sure nobody sees them drop those bags off," Eric told Pistol Pete. All of the bricks that were left in the Cadillac truck from the job they had done a few days ago, Eric was going to stash them in the five hotel rooms that were off limits that way just in case something ever went wrong he always had a backup plan.

Eric hung around the hotel making small talk as he watched one of his men enter the hotel every ten minutes carrying a duffle bag not to draw attention to the situation. Each man was told to act as if they had never seen Eric before in their lives and they did just that.

An hour later, Eric sat in the back seat of his B.M.W while, Pistol Pete drove him home. Eric had a lot on his mind and needed to lay down and get some rest. Ever since he began involving himself in the family business, it seemed as if he was stressed all the time now. He was no longer happy and enjoying life, everything was always life and death. Eric had to make sure he stayed one-step ahead of everyone, one mistake and he could lose his freedom forever.

"You alright back there?" Pistol Pete asked glancing at Eric through the rear view mirror.

"I'm good," Eric replied. "Hey Pete, I just wanted to say thank you for always watching over me and making sure I'm safe out here."

Pistol Pete nodded his head. "I'm just doing my job. A long time ago your mother Millie saved my life this is the least I could do."

"My mother has been out of my life for a long time now due to her current situation," Eric said. "How was she before she caught her case?"

"Millie was and will always be a wonderful woman," Pistol Pete began. "She's straight forward and as loyal as they come. She's also the smartest businesswoman I've ever met. Put it this way, I would love to have a woman like Millie in my corner."

Eric smiled after hearing such wonderful things about his mother. He missed Millie a lot and he was counting down the couple of months she had left on her bid. The B.M.W. pulled up in front of Eric's house when he noticed Kelly's Range Rover parked out front.

Eric stepped out of his B.M.W and saw Kelly standing in front of the front door. "What are you doing here, Kelly?"

"I need to talk to you," Kelly said with a sad look in her eyes. Her clothes were wrinkled and looked as if they had been slept in for the past three days. Her hair looked as if she had just raked it with her fingers.

Eric opened the front door and let Kelly inside, then turned and faced Pistol Pete. "Take the rest of the night off. I have to talk to my wife for a second."

"Eric I'm sorry if I hurt you," Kelly began. "I know you probably don't ever want to see me again but I just want you to know that I love you with all my heart and I'm sorry."

"Why are you here?"

"I came over to ask you could I take a shower," Kelly said as tears ran down her eyes. She had no family and nowhere to go; her family turned their backs on her years ago for dating a black man that family was well known for being criminals. Now she had nobody.

"Why does it look like you've been sleeping in your car?" Eric asked.

"Eric I have no money and nowhere to stay. You threw me out with just the clothes I had on my back, I don't even have money to get a hotel room," Kelly wiped the tears from her face.

"Go take a shower, Kelly," Eric removed his suit jacket, sat his gun down on the counter, and poured himself a drink.

"Do I still have clothes in the closet or did you throw them all out?"

"All of your things are still here," Eric said with his back turned to her. He sipped his drink as he heard Kelly make her way upstairs. He hated, Kelly's guts but a part of him still felt badly for her. At the end of the day, she was still his wife and he didn't want to see her doing bad.

Fifteen minutes later, Kelly made her way back downstairs dressed in some clean clothes and her blonde hair pulled back into a ponytail. "Thank you, Eric."

"You're welcome."

Kelly headed for the front door when she heard, Eric say, "You don't have to leave."

"Huh?"

"You don't have to leave," Eric repeated. "I mean this is your house too."

"Thank you so much, Eric," Kelly said. She was so thankful that, Eric had allowed her back into the house.

"You hungry?"

Kelly nodded her head. "Yes."

JACK MASON

43

Jack smiled as he stood in the warehouse full of work. He had never seen this much drugs at one time in his life. Jack had gotten a tip that Jimmy had just filled an entire apartment building with product. It was a genius idea for the Mason Family to buy an entire apartment building and use all the apartments as stash houses. Jack sent a team of killers in the apartment building to retrieve all the drugs in the entire building. At the end of the day, twelve men were murdered in total and Jack was now the owner of the product.

Jack walked over to, Black. "I want this product on the streets before the night is out, we going to slowly take over Derrick's territory one block at a time."

"I'm on top of it," Black said. "Now that we have all of their product do you want me to pull our people off of the family?"

"No," Jack said quickly. "I still want every last one of them dead." Jack knew that once word got back to the

Mason Family that he was the one taking over their territory that an all-out war was sure to follow. So he figured he might as well eliminate the problem now before it's too late.

"What about Mike," Black, asked. He wasn't too fond at the thought of killing a cop.

"Don't worry about Mike. I'll handle him," Jack said as he hopped in his car and exited the warehouse. Jack cruised down the highway and smiled at the thought of how much money he was about to be making. He hated that he had to go this route, but what other choices did he have? He had already came to Derrick multiple times asking for a spot on the team and every time he was denied. Jack pulled up to a block that belonged to Derrick. He removed a 9mm from under the seat, screwed a silencer onto the barrel, and stepped out the car. Jack walked straight up to the two men that stood on the corner and blew the first man's head off. His partner quickly took off in a sprint. Seconds later, he crashed down to the concrete face first with two bullet holes in his back. Jack walked off, got back into his car, and pulled away from the crime scene.

JIMMY

44

"I'm sorry baby," Jimmy said as he pushed Stoney's wheelchair through the front door. When the doctor told Jimmy that Stoney would never walk again, it crushed him on the inside. Jimmy felt responsible for her being in that chair. The gunmen were out to kill him and unfortunately, Stoney just happened to be with him.

"It's not your fault," Stoney said in a light whisper. She still couldn't believe that she had been shot it all felt like one bad dream and Stoney couldn't wait to wake up. She tried her hardest to move her legs but nothing happened. "Why me?" She whispered.

"What you say baby?"

"I said why me!" Stoney yelled as tears ran down her face. "I don't deserve to be in this fucking chair. You should be the one in this chair those bullets were meant for you not me!" Stoney said through clenched teeth.

"Baby I'm sorry."

"Is sorry going to make me walk again? Huh? Is sorry going to take the bullets back? Is sorry going to get me out of this fucking chair?" Stoney yelled. At the moment, she hated Jimmy's guts and couldn't stand to even look at him. In her heart, Stoney felt as if Jimmy should have protected her. "If you would have never came to my job being jealous I would still be able to walk right now."

"I know you're upset right now baby," Jimmy said trying to calm Stoney down. "I promise I will find whoever is responsible for this."

"And then what?" Stoney snapped. "You killing them is never going to make me be able to walk again."

"What do you want me to do? I said I was sorry."

"You can take your sorry and shove it up your ass!" Stoney said with venom dripping from her voice.

Jimmy shook his head as he answered his ringing cell phone. "Yeah what's up? When right now? You gotta be fucking kidding me! I'm on my way!" Jimmy ended the call and headed for the door. "I'll be back in a little while," he said and made his exit.

* * *

Jimmy pulled up in front of the apartment building where the product was stashed. He had gotten a call about eight of his men getting gunned down and the entire stash being taken. "Tell me this is a joke?" Jimmy said to the soldier that stood out front waiting for him.

"I'm afraid not," the soldier said escorting Jimmy inside the building so he could see how bad the damage was for himself.

"Any word on who's behind this?" Jimmy asked. "I want a name."

"Working on that now but honestly this had to be an inside job," the worker told, Jimmy. "Only people in the Mason circle knew about this place only soldiers with rank had knowledge about this spot."

Jimmy thought about how many people knew about the stash building and off the top of his head he could only think of maybe nine people with knowledge that the place even exist. "Narrow it down and get back to it I want a name within forty eight hours."

MIKE

45

"The Mason Family has brought an entire apartment building to stash their drugs," The captain began. "Something went wrong and a few members of their crew wound up getting their heads blown off and robbed," he paused for a second. "Thank god because now we have a warrant to search the apartment building as well as all of the other businesses owned by the Mason Family. The mayor has given us the green light and all the resources we need to take the entire Mason Family down. Right now, Derrick Mason is laying up in a hospital bed I want enough evidence so that once it's time for him to be released from the hospital we'll be right there to arrest him and put him in jail for the rest of his life," the captain smiled. "Any questions?"

"Yes when do we get started?" Mike asked. "I can't wait to get started and arrest these scumbags." He said laying it on thick for all of his coworkers. The news on the family being robbed was news to him as well he had been so caught up in his regular job that he hadn't had time to keep up on the family business. He had no idea what Derrick's status was he told himself that as soon as he had a free moment he was going to call Jimmy so he could get pulled up to speed.

"We get started today and Mike, I assigned you to be the team lead everyone will be following your orders," the captain said. "Are you excited to be a part of bringing down the infamous Mason Family?"

"I'm elated," Mike said, forcing a fake smile on his face. He could already see that there was no way that this was going to end well.

JACK MASON

46

Jack stepped out of his vehicle and walked towards the front door with Black close on his heels. Everything was going according to plan; he was making plenty of money now and slowly but surely taking over Derrick's territory one block at a time. Jack was building a strong team of shooters and killers getting prepared for the war that was sure to come. With the type of money Jack was making he felt untouchable, felt as if he was on top of the world. He felt like he was above the law. He made sure the first thing he did was put a couple of police officers on his payroll to make sure that things ran smoothly. Jack wanted to make sure that he was prepared for any and everything that could be thrown his way. Jack raised his finger and rang the doorbell. He heard movement on the other side of the door finally the door swung open and a beautiful woman in a wheel chair answered the door in a nasty mood. "Can I help you?

"Yes, is Jimmy home?" Jack asked politely. He was tired of sending boys to do a man's job. He lived by the motto if you want something done right then you do it yourself.

"No he's not home right now."

"Are you home alone?" Jack asked trying to peek inside the house.

"I said he's not home right now," Stoney said. She went to slam the door but Jack forced his way inside the house. "What the fuck you think you doing?"

Jack turned and slapped Stoney across her face so hard that one of her earrings flew out of her ear and her wheelchair tip over. Jack put his foot on Stoney's neck, removed his .357 from his holster, and aimed it at her head. "Tell me where I can find Jimmy."

"I don't know where he is. He got a phone call and left," Stoney told the two men.

"You got five seconds to tell me where I can find Jimmy or else I'm going to shoot you in your face." Jack threatened.

Stoney chuckled. "Motherfucker I'm never going to walk again my life is already over do what you gotta because I ain't telling you shit!"

Jack squeezed the trigger and watched as Stoney's face splatter all over the hard wood floor. "We out," Jack said as him and Black made their exit.

Black got in the car, put his seat belt on, turned, and looked at Jack. "What's next?"

"Now we head to Eric Mason's house." Jack replied.

DERRICK

47

Derrick laid on his hospital bed catching up on some much needed rest. Doctors told him that he would be fine and would be able to return home in a few days but for now, he needed to rest. The pills that the nurses gave Derrick helped him sleep and made his pain temporarily go away.

Derrick was counting sheep when all of a sudden his eyes snapped open when he heard the sound of a machine gun being fired. He sat up and wiped his eyes thinking that maybe he had been dreaming but when he saw his bodyguards hop up from the chair that rested down by the foot of his bed and run out into the hallway with a gun in his hand he realized that this was real. Derrick sat in his bed with a scared look on his face as the sound of multiple machine guns could be heard ringing out. Whoever had attempted to kill Derrick the first time was back to finish the job. Derrick winced as he reached over and snatched out all the tubes and wires that were all hooked up to machines. He slowly guided his legs off the bed and slowly eased his way over to the door. Derrick was moving as slow as a snail but at the moment that was as fast as his body allowed him to move. He snatched his room door open and saw dead bodies sprawled all throughout the hallway. Derrick quickly reached down and removed the gun from the cop who was guarding his door holster. The sound of the loud gunfire seemed to be getting louder and louder which meant whoever was coming for Derrick was getting closer and closer. Derrick limped down the hall as fast as he could, when he heard the gunfire stop he knew he had ran out of time. "Shit!" He cursed as he heard the sound of several men in combat boots making their way down the hall at a fast pace. Derrick quickly entered the first room he saw on his left. He entered the room, placed his back to the wall, and aimed his gun at the door. If Derrick was going out he promised himself that he wasn't going alone. Derrick's palms began to sweat as he heard the footsteps stop directly in front of the door of the room that he was in. "Come on motherfucker open the door," he whispered to himself. "Open the door."

Derrick saw the knob move as the door eased open. Without thinking twice, he pulled the trigger.

Boom!

TO BE CONTINUED...

Books by Good2Go Authors on Our Bookshelf

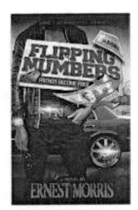

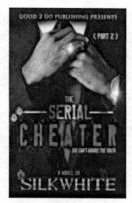

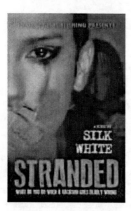

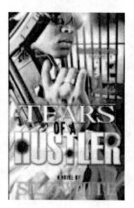

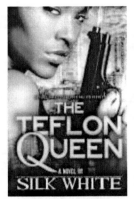

Good 2 Go Films Presents

To order books, please fill out the order form below:

To order films please go to *www.good2gofilms.com*

Name:_____

Address:_____

City: _____ State: _____ Zip Code: _____

Phone:_____

Email:_____

Method of Payment: Check   VISA   MASTERCARD

Credit Card#:_____

Name as it appears on card: _____

Signature: _____

Item Name	Price	Qty	Amount
48 Hours to Die – Silk White	$14.99		
Business Is Business – Silk White	$14.99		
Business Is Business 2 – Silk White	$14.99		
Flipping Numbers – Ernest Morris	$14.99		
Flipping Numbers 2 – Ernest Morris	$14.99		
He Loves Me, He Loves You Not - Mychea	$14.99		
He Loves Me, He Loves You Not 2 - Mychea	$14.99		
He Loves Me, He Loves You Not 3 - Mychea	$14.99		
He Loves Me, He Loves You Not 4 - Mychea	$14.99		
Married To Da Streets – Silk White	$14.99		
My Besties – Asia Hill	$14.99		
My Besties 2 – Asia Hill	$14.99		
My Boyfriend's Wife - Mychea	$14.99		
Never Be The Same – Silk White	$14.99		
Stranded – Silk White	$14.99		
Slumped – Jason Brent	$14.99		
Tears of a Hustler - Silk White	$14.99		
Tears of a Hustler 2 - Silk White	$14.99		
Tears of a Hustler 3 - Silk White	$14.99		
Tears of a Hustler 4- Silk White	$14.99		
Tears of a Hustler 5 – Silk White	$14.99		
Tears of a Hustler 6 – Silk White	$14.99		
The Panty Ripper - Reality Way	$14.99		
The Panty Ripper 3 – Reality Way	$14.99		
The Teflon Queen – Silk White	$14.99		
The Teflon Queen 2 – Silk White	$14.99		

The Teflon Queen 3 – Silk White	$14.99		
The Teflon Queen 4 – Silk White	$14.99		
Time Is Money - Silk White	$14.99		
Young Goonz – Reality Way	$14.99		
Subtotal:			
Tax:			
Shipping (Free) U.S. Media Mail:			
Total:			

Make Checks Payable To:
Good2Go Publishing
7311 W Glass Lane,
Laveen, AZ 85339

CPSIA information can be obtained at www.ICGtesting.com
Printed in the USA
LVOW07s2133310715

448461LV00007B/40/P

9 780990 869474